Who could resist this man?

Amy looked at Quinn, standing there with his dark hair shining in the light from the streetlamp. He had been her knight in shining armor tonight, riding up out of nowhere and vanquishing her enemies. Her heart swelled with old, foolish emotions.

Even though it wasn't the smartest thing to do given her unrequited crush, Amy pressed a kiss to Quinn's cheek. His arms came around her, and the next thing she knew she was clamped against his chest. His wool coat was as soft as silk beneath her hands, his body beneath it big and strong. Amy closed her eyes and inhaled the smell of expensive wool and subtle, woody aftershave.

A rush of warm emotion washed over her. One look, one touch and she was thinking about all the things she'd never have. It was too hard. Too cruel. Yet still she wanted him.

Dear Reader,

This book was inspired by my good friend Helen's recounting of how she and her husband moved from friends to lovers. They were renovating an old theater, and through the long hours of talking and working together they fell in love. Naturally, such a great real-life story got my imagination ticking over. When I closed my eyes, however, I kept picturing an old cinema rather than a playhouse, and thus the Grand Picture Theatre was born.

I have always loved Art Deco architecture. There are some truly amazing old cinemas in my home town of Melbourne, and when I visited Florence, Italy, a few years ago I fell in love with the Odeon Cinehall, a stunning Art Nouveau cinema that just took my breath away. If you are ever in that neck of the woods, I highly recommend a visit—they play lots of English language movies and watching a film there makes you feel like royalty.

I hope you enjoy Quinn and Amy's story. I love hearing from readers, and you can find my e-mail address at my Web site, www.sarahmayberry.com.

Until next time,

Sarah Mayberry

Her Best Friend
Sarah Mayberry

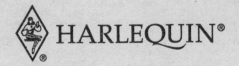

TORONTO • NEW YORK • LONDON
AMSTERDAM • PARIS • SYDNEY • HAMBURG
STOCKHOLM • ATHENS • TOKYO • MILAN • MADRID
PRAGUE • WARSAW • BUDAPEST • AUCKLAND

Recycling programs
for this product may
not exist in your area.

ISBN-13: 978-0-373-71626-5

HER BEST FRIEND

Printed in U.S.A.

ABOUT THE AUTHOR

Sarah Mayberry lives in Melbourne, Australia, with her partner, who is also a writer. When she's not gazing off into space thinking about the characters in her latest story, she loves going to the movies, yoga, meditation and shoe shopping (not neccessarily in that order!). She's hoping that by the time you read this she will be the proud owner of a new puppy—breed yet to be decided.

Books by Sarah Mayberry

HARLEQUIN SUPERROMANCE

1551—A NATURAL FATHER
1599—HOME FOR THE HOLIDAYS

HARLEQUIN BLAZE

380—BURNING UP
404—BELOW THE BELT
425—AMOROUS LIAISONS
464—SHE'S GOT IT BAD
517—HER SECRET FLING

This book would not exist if I did not have Chris by my side.

Having his story smarts and endless patience on my side makes all the difference. Love you.

I also want to thank Helen for sharing the story of her real-life romance with me—thanks for giving me Amy and Quinn!

And last, but never least, thanks to Wanda. Bless the day I ended up on your desk.

CHAPTER ONE

AMY PARKER SLOWED her steps as she approached the Grand Picture Theatre. The setting sun painted the old cinema's crumbling white Spanish Mission facade pink and apricot, and for a moment—if she squinted and really used her imagination—she could picture the Grand as it had once been: elegant, beautiful, a testament to a bygone era.

Four more days.

Then the sale contract would be signed off and the Grand would be hers and she could start making the image in her mind a reality.

Amy stepped closer to the double glass doors at the entrance. The front windows had been covered with newspaper for years, but a section on the right door had peeled away. She stood on her toes and shaded her eyes with her hands so she could see through the gap. Inside, the marble parquet tiles were dull with dirt and grime while crumpled newspaper, old boxes and dust balls dotted the floor. The once stunning concession stand was scarred with age, the mirrors behind it tarnished and chipped. It would take weeks to set things right in there. And the foyer was the least of her problems. Way down on her To Do list.

The roof needed fixing, the stucco on the facade had

to be renewed. The plumbing was shot and the whole of the interior smelled of damp and mold. She had her work cut out for her, that was for sure.

She smiled. She couldn't freaking wait.

"Amy. There you are. I tried you at the store but your mother said you'd left already."

It was Reg Hanover, council chairman. Even though he was wearing yet another of his truly hideous ties, she beamed at him. On Friday, this portly middle-aged man and his fellow council members would be signing over the Grand to her in exchange for her hard-won savings and a sizable bank loan. Right now, she loved him, ugly tie and all.

"Reg. Hey there. I was just drooling," she said. "Prematurely, I know. But I couldn't help myself."

Reg's face was pink from the walk from her parents' hardware store.

"Yes. Well. About that." He cleared his throat and smoothed a hand down his tie. This one was beige, with a picture of a black horse rearing on it. Really bad, even for Reg.

She shifted her attention to his face. There was something about the way he couldn't quite make himself meet her eyes. And the way he kept swallowing nervously.

"Is there some kind of problem?"

"Amy, there's no point in beating around the bush. I'm just going to say it—we've had another offer. And we're going to take it."

Amy blinked a few times, trying to make sense of his words. "I don't understand."

"Ulrich Construction has come in with a last-minute offer. The council needs to think of the whole community, and we believe this is the best outcome for everyone."

He sounded stiff, as though he'd been rehearsing his speech in his mind.

"But we had a deal. A contract."

"No, Amy, we had a conversation. A conversation is not legally binding."

She gaped. She couldn't believe he was being so slippery.

"We negotiated a contract, Reg. I have a copy at home. You were going to sign it at this week's meeting."

"I'm sorry, but we had a better deal come in, and we took it. I know you're disappointed, but that's the way these things go."

He checked his watch then glanced up the street, as though he had better things to do than break her heart.

"Have you signed off on the deal yet?" she asked.

"No, but we will on Friday."

"I want to talk to the other councillors," she said, crossing her arms over her chest and lifting her chin.

"Fine. They'll all be at the meeting. Members of the public are welcome."

Members of the public? Yesterday the council had been ready to sign over ownership of the Grand to her and today she was a *member of the public?*

She was still trying to find something to say that didn't contain the words *sneaky rat fink* when Reg reached out and patted her arm.

"It's probably for the best. It was unlikely you were ever going to be able to restore this big old place on your own, anyway."

He walked away. Amy stared at his retreating back. She was at a loss as to how to respond, how to feel, what to think.

For more than ten years she'd lived and breathed the dream of buying the old theatre that her great-grandfather had built. She'd lain awake on more nights than she could count regilding the decorative moldings in her mind, reupholstering the sectional seating, polishing the floors, imagining how glorious it could all be if she could only scrape together the money to purchase the theatre from the local council.

She'd invested the small legacy her grandparents had left her and saved her wages from working in her parents' hardware store and taken any extra work that had come her way, planning for the day when she'd have enough for a deposit.

And finally she'd made it. At least she'd thought she had.

The shock was beginning to wear off. She didn't understand how another offer could come out of the blue. The Grand had been an eyesore on the main street of the small Victoria, Australia town of Daylesford for years. It had ceased operating as a cinema in the eighties and had been empty for a long time, ever since the antiques dealer who'd been renting the space had found better premises. No one except Amy had seemed to give a toss about the old place. And yet suddenly the Grand was a hot ticket?

She needed to know more. She pulled out her cell phone and dialed her friend Denise, who worked at the municipal office. If anyone knew the details of this other offer, it would be her.

"'Nise, it's me. I need some inside info. But only if it won't get you in trouble."

"Fire away. I'm all yours, babe," Denise said.

"Ulrich Construction has put in a last-minute bid on the Grand. I need to know what their prop says."

"But the Grand is yours! I typed up your contract myself."

"It's not signed yet, 'Nise."

"Oh. Crap. The meeting's this week, isn't it? Give me five minutes, I'll call you back."

Amy paced in front of the Grand while she waited, arms crossed over her chest. It was late April and it was getting darker and colder by the minute, but she didn't care. She wasn't leaving this spot until she knew for sure what was going on. That her dream really was over.

Seven minutes later, her phone rang. It was Denise, and when she told Amy what she'd discovered, Amy literally felt dizzy with shock.

Ulrich Construction wanted to buy the Grand and knock down everything but the facade, replacing it with a four-story apartment block. They wanted to destroy the intricate plasterwork on the domed ceiling inside the theatre, smash the marble stairway to the balcony section, scrap the Murano glass wall sconces. They would pay lip service to preserving the Grand while wiping out everything that made the theatre so unique.

"You want me to come pick you up and pour some wine into you?" Denise offered when Amy was silent for too long.

"No. Thanks for this, 'Nise. I have to go."

Amy ended the call and pressed her palm against her forehead.

She needed to think. She needed to get past the panic that was making her heart race and her stomach churn.

She needed a lawyer.

Yes. Absolutely. That was definitely the first step. She needed a smart, sharp mouthpiece in a suit. Someone formidable who could arm her with the necessary information.

She started searching her phone contacts for a number she hadn't dialed in months.

There had been good reasons for that, of course. Sensible, sanity preserving reasons. But this was an emergency. All bets were off. Her old school friend Lisa dealt with property law all the time in Sydney. She'd know how to handle this. She'd tell Amy if there was any way she could stop this disaster from happening.

Amy found the number as an unwelcome thought slunk into her mind: *What if Quinn answers instead of Lisa?*

Amy froze, staring at the number on the screen.

After all these years, she still couldn't think of Quinn Whitfield without feeling a skip of excitement, closely followed by a thump of dread.

Dumb. And dangerous. He was married. *They* were married. Her two best friends.

Which was why she'd been deliberately trying to distance herself recently. Not returning phone calls. Being lazy with e-mails. Freezing them out.

But it wasn't as though she'd gone to school with a million lawyers. It was either Lisa or a lawyer chosen at random from the phone book—an arrangement that would come complete with a hefty bill her tight restoration budget could not afford.

Hopefully Lisa would pick up and not Quinn. And if it was him…well, Amy would deal with it. She pressed the button and listened as the phone rang.

Come on, Lisa, pick up. Pick up, pick up, pick up.

A click sounded and suddenly Quinn's voice was in her ear. Her stomach tensed—then she realized it was only a recording.

"Hi, there. You've called the Whitfields. We can't get to the phone right now. Leave a message and your contact details and we'll do our best to get back to you as soon as we can. Unless you're selling life insurance, then you know what you can do."

It had been nearly eighteen months since she'd spoken to Quinn, but he sounded exactly the same. She could even imagine the slight smile he would have been wearing when he recorded the message. Self-aware, wry. Charming as all hell.

The answering machine beeped and she took a quick breath.

"Lisa and, um, Quinn. Long time no speak, huh? Lis, I was actually calling to talk to you. I need some legal advice and it's kind of urgent—"

"Amy. Hey. How the hell are you?"

Amy's heart banged against her rib cage as Quinn's deep voice sounded down the line. Not a recording this time. The real thing.

"Quinn. Hi."

She closed her eyes. He sounded so *good*. And so pleased to hear from her.

And why not? She'd been the "best person" at his wedding. They'd grown up next door to each other. He'd taught her how to fish, and she'd taught him the best way to climb the apple tree at the bottom of her parents' yard. They'd learned to ride their bikes together, and they'd been punished together any number of times for too many pranks to count. Rotten eggs in the air-conditioning vent at school. Releasing Quinn's pet ferret in class. Filling the neighbor's exhaust pipe with water from the garden hose.

Their exploits had been legendary. Then Lisa moved to town the year of Amy's fourteenth birthday, and everything changed.

"I'm good, thanks. How about you?" she said.

"Keeping body and soul together. Man, it's been a long time since I heard your voice."

"Yeah." She swallowed the lump in her throat. Wondered if he guessed she'd been deliberately pushing him away, or if he thought it was just time and distance that had come between them.

"I was thinking about you the other day, actually," he said.

She'd been about to ask if Lisa was home, but his words caught her by surprise. "Really?"

"Yeah. I was thinking about the wedding. The night before, actually. How you and I went down to the lake and drank all that beer. Remember?"

"I remember."

How could she forget? She'd matched him beer for beer, desperate to prolong every last second with him before he stopped being her best friend and became one half of Mr. and Mrs. Quinn and Lisa Whitfield.

Would it have been easier if Lisa hadn't been her close friend, the third musketeer? Would it have hurt as much if Quinn had fallen for a stranger from out of town?

Amy would never know.

She pinched the bridge of her nose. This was why she'd hesitated over calling. So many memories, all washing over her.

Time to get this conversation back on track.

"Listen, I, um, don't want to keep you too long. Is Lisa around? I need to ask her advice on a legal thing."

There was a short pause as Quinn registered the abrupt shift in conversation. She'd been too sharp, too quick to cut him off. She held her breath, waiting for him to ask the questions that were bubbling beneath the surface of their conversation.

Why did you stop returning my calls?
Why aren't we friends anymore?
What did I do wrong?

"Lisa's not around at the moment. Is it anything I can help with?"

"It's fine. I'll wait for her to call me back."

"What's the problem, Ames? Lisa might have gotten better marks than me but I made partner before her." Quinn was joking, but there was an edge to his tone.

Because, of course, Quinn was a lawyer, too. One of the many things he and Lisa had in common. He could just as easily answer her questions, yet Amy had made a point of asking for Lisa, of thinking of Lisa and not him when she'd realized she needed legal advice.

"It's not that. I didn't want to bother you," she said quickly.

"But you're happy to bother Lisa?"

Because I haven't been in love with Lisa for more years than I can count. Because talking to her doesn't make me think about all the hours I've spent aching over you, wishing you loved me instead of her. Making myself sick with jealousy and guilt and lust.

"No. It's just we haven't spoken for a while, and I don't want to be one of those fair-weather friends who calls out of the blue and hits you up for a favor because I need some legal advice."

Quinn made an impatient noise. "For Pete's sake, Amy. We grew up together. You're my oldest friend. Tell me the problem."

She hesitated a moment longer. But he was right. She was being stupid. She'd always been stupid where Quinn was concerned.

"I've been negotiating with the council for the past

few months to buy the Grand. We have a contract all ready to go—"

"Whoa. Hold on a second. You finally got the money together to buy the Grand?"

"That's what I said."

"Ames. That's fantastic. What an amazing achievement."

It scared her how much his praise meant to her, how much it made her chest ache.

"Well, I'm not there yet."

"Right. You've got a contract…?" he prompted.

Over the next few minutes she briefed him on the situation. It made her feel sick and angry all over again as she thought about the peremptory way Reg Hanover had delivered the news. As though she was a pesky child to be shooed from the room.

"If the contract wasn't signed, there's not much you can do to hold them to the agreement. You know that, right?" Quinn said.

"This isn't about my contract. I need to know if there's anything I can do to protect the Grand. It's on the town's heritage register. Surely that means Ulrich can't knock it down?"

Her voice broke on the last few words and she felt immeasurably foolish.

"You okay?"

"Yes."

"I'm going to need some time to do a bit of research, find out more about the local heritage register and council bylaws. In some municipalities, what Ulrich is proposing is acceptable—a compromise between heritage preservation and commerce. Can I get back to you?"

"Of course."

"Probably won't be until tomorrow morning, okay?"

"Sure."

"Try not to freak out in the meantime."

"Too late. And thanks, Quinn."

She could almost see his shrug, even though he was hundreds of miles away. "No worries, Ames."

He ended the call. She slid her phone into her pocket and started walking to her car.

She hadn't spoken to Quinn for months, had dodged his phone calls and avoided responding to his e-mails. And he'd responded to her request for help without hesitation. Without question.

It was one of the things she'd always loved about him the most: his generosity. But then there had always been a lot to love about Quinn Whitfield. His clever mind. His kindness. His sense of humor. Then there was his body— tall and broad and strong....

Stop it. Stop it before you're right back at the same old place again.

She had bigger fish to fry than lost loves and old regrets. It was far better to channel her energy into a battle she at least had a chance of winning.

Because she'd lost Quinn long ago.

QUINN SAT QUIETLY for a moment after he'd hung up the phone.

For the first few seconds of the call he'd thought Amy was calling because she knew, because his mother had let something slip or Lisa had made contact to tell her the big news.

But Amy hadn't known. And he hadn't told her.

"I'm going home now, Mr. Whitfield."

Quinn glanced up to see Maria hovering in the doorway of his study.

"Okay. Thanks. I'll see you in a few weeks," he said.

"You have a good holiday, okay?" she said. "You work too hard. You need to rest."

"I will. You enjoy your break, too."

She waved her hand as though he was talking nonsense. He knew she cleaned a number of houses as well as his own. She probably never stopped working.

"And maybe you should try to eat some more while you're away," she said.

"I'll do what I can."

She gave him a last wave before disappearing and he let the easy smile fade from his lips. She was worried about him, just as they'd been worried about him at the office. Lots of hushed conversations about "poor Quinn" and how he was working too late and how much weight he'd lost. Hence the holiday. Two weeks up north on Hamilton Island, whether he liked it or not.

"Take some time off, Quinn. Look after yourself. No one expects you to be a machine," his boss had said.

Not an order, but close enough.

Quinn sighed and raked a hand through his hair. At the moment, work was his solace. He had no idea what he'd do without it. Face the wreckage of his marriage, he supposed.

Hard to get too enthusiastic about that.

Even though his leave had officially started this morning, he'd been tidying up loose ends at home, and he saved the last draft of the Monroe contract before sending a quick e-mail to his assistant to let her know it was ready to be released to the client. Then he glanced down at the notes he'd made while talking to Amy.

He still couldn't believe she was in a position to buy the Grand, after all these years. And that he hadn't known about it.

She'd been obsessed with the place since they were kids. Used to drag him past it as they walked home from school every day, even though it was out of their way. It had been a clothing clearance store back then, the cinema having gone out of business years before. He used to wait beside the door while she made her way through the racks of seconds and the previous year's fashions to stand with her head tilted back as she studied the elaborate plaster ceiling high above. He could still remember how she used to wrap her arms around her midsection as she drank it all in, as though she was scared her excitement would get away from her if she didn't keep a grip on herself.

It felt wrong that she'd reached such a significant milestone in her life and he'd known nothing about it. But then he'd been hanging on to some pretty big news of his own, hadn't he? He could hardly fault her when he'd just failed to tell her that he was getting a divorce.

He called up an online search engine. Given a choice, he'd rather work than contemplate his navel. Every time.

An hour later he'd accessed the local council Web site and downloaded the relevant bylaws. He'd also tracked down some recent decisions on heritage protections in the Victorian Supreme Court. It was nearly eight and his stomach was hollow with hunger. He walked to the take-out Indian restaurant on the corner and bought a chicken curry he probably wouldn't finish.

It was cool out and he tugged the collar of his leather jacket higher on his neck as he walked back home. Two-storied Victorian terrace houses marched down either side of the street, their balconies decorated with elaborate wrought iron lacework. He stopped in front of his own terrace house, taking a moment to note the clean white paint and the glossy black trim. Wisteria climbed one of the balcony supports, and the front garden was a masterpiece of precise hedges and rounded topiary.

He'd been so proud of this place when they'd signed the papers two years ago. A little scared, too, of the debt they'd been taking on. But Lisa had sold him on the risk, convinced him that they needed to live in the right suburb, drive the right kind of cars, have the right people over for dinner. She'd always been ambitious. Keen to kick the dust of small-town Australia off her heels. It was one of the things he'd always admired about her.

He hadn't realized that she'd outgrow him one day, too.

He walked up the path to the front door and slid his key into the lock. He braced himself, then pushed the door open. And there it was—a wash of jasmine and spice. Lisa's perfume, even though she'd been gone for nearly a year. He caught an echo of it every time he came home. Something he could definitely live without.

He walked to the kitchen, dumping his dinner on the counter before crossing to the rear of the house and flinging the French doors wide open. The house needed airing out, that was the problem.

He upended his curry into a bowl and grabbed a fork from the drawer. Once the divorce was finalized, this place would go on the market and he wouldn't have to worry about her perfume anymore. Then he could move to an apartment, maybe some place in the city. A bachelor pad, full of high-tech gadgets and the kind of non-fussy furniture he preferred.

Quinn stared down at the messy curry in his bowl. This was not how he'd imagined his life would look at thirty. Not by a long shot.

He took his dinner to the study and immersed himself in the work he was doing for Amy. Another hour of research and digging and he had the information he needed to help her with her cause. He picked up the phone, then put it down again without dialing.

There was something he needed to get straight with himself before he spoke to her again. He'd lied to her earlier when she'd asked if Lisa was there, leading her to believe that Lisa was out for the evening rather than long gone. Which went far beyond simply not telling her the marriage was over.

Why hadn't he told her, the way he'd told his parents and his colleagues at work and his and Lisa's mutual friends here in Sydney?

He rubbed the bridge of his nose. Leaned back in his chair.

The truth was, he hadn't wanted his oldest friend to know that his marriage was a failure. Which was a great gauge for where his head was at the moment, wasn't it?

Maybe he really did need this holiday.

He hadn't been lying when he told Amy that he'd been thinking about her, though. He'd been thinking about her a lot. About the conversations they used to have lying in the tall grass at the bottom of her parents' yard. About the way she always used to call him on his bullshit. About the times all three of them, he and Amy and Lisa, had gone swimming in the lake after dark.

All of it a far cry from the polished, finely honed world he occupied now. The corner office. The partnership in the prestigious law firm. The expensive European car. The soon-to-be expensive divorce.

Quinn shook his head. He really needed to get his head out of his own ass. Too much time on his own these days and he started thinking things to death. This was why he worked late. And why he was reluctant to spend two weeks on an island somewhere pretending to read a spy novel.

He palmed the phone and dialed Amy's cell. She answered after one ring and he knew she'd probably been hovering by the damned thing, hoping he'd call back, even though he'd said it wouldn't be until morning.

"Quinn," she said. She sounded breathless. Scared.

"Good news. I've done some digging, and the Grand is listed on the town's heritage register for both its interior and exterior architectural features. Which means that any development has to preserve the interior as well as the facade."

"Oh my God. Thank you. Oh, Quinn. Thank you." Her voice was thick with emotion.

"Don't get too excited yet. Ulrich's proposal shouldn't have ever made it past first base. But it did, which means council are prepared to flout their own bylaws if given enough incentive."

There was a long silence from the other end of the phone.

"But once I point out that they can't do that, they'll have to reject the offer, right?" Amy said.

"Not if they think they can get away with it. If the money's big enough, people will do just about anything, Amy. I've been doing some checking, and Ulrich Construction has the contract to build the extension on the school gym, the new wing on the library and the new medical center over near the day spa. I'd say Barry Ulrich and the council are very nicely tucked up in bed with each other, wouldn't you?"

"Oh." She sounded nonplussed, and despite the seriousness of the situation, he had to smile. Amy had always been too busy thinking the best of people to see the worst.

"The council was probably hoping that they could slip this under the radar while nobody was looking."

"Well, that's not going to happen," she said. "Not while I'm still living and breathing."

"I didn't think so."

"So, what do I do? Go to the meeting, let them know that I know what they're up to?" He could hear her taking notes.

"For starters. Take people with you, make sure there are plenty of witnesses to keep the councillors on their toes."

"Dad can get his cronies from the Chamber of Commerce to come along. They can throw a bit of weight around when they want to. And Denise knows a guy at the local paper."

"Perfect. I'll draft up a statement for you to read. Something with enough legalese in it to give them pause."

"Good. Pause is just what I want to give them. And then some."

"I'm heading off on holiday tomorrow, but I'll get the statement to you by morning, okay? And you can reach me on my cell if you need me."

"Oh. Okay." There was a short silence. "Where are you guys going?"

Now was the time to correct her, tell her that he was going on holiday alone. That Lisa had left him.

"Hamilton Island. Couple of weeks of sun and surf."

"Sounds good."

He drew a meaningless squiggle on the page in front of him. "Yeah."

She took a deep breath on the other end of the line. "You've been great, Quinn. I want you to know I really appreciate your help with this."

24 · HER BEST FRIEND

"It's no big deal, Ames."

"It is to me. It's a huge deal."

"Well." He made another squiggle, then obliterated it in a flurry of pen strokes. "Don't be a stranger, okay? Drop me a line now and then. And let me know how things go on Friday, okay?"

"I will."

Neither of them said anything for a long moment. He could hear her breathing and he could feel the truth pushing its way up his throat.

It's all screwed, Ames. My marriage, my life. I have no idea what I'm doing anymore.

"Good luck," he said. Then he put the phone down before the truth could escape.

She didn't want to hear his sad story. She was fighting for her dream. And they weren't friends the way they used to be. He'd done something wrong, or something had gone wrong and he'd been too busy with his own crap to notice.

Same difference.

He flicked off the lights and walked through his empty house.

OVER THE NEXT THREE DAYS, Amy cajoled, begged, bribed and harassed her friends and neighbors until they agreed to join her at the council meeting on Friday evening. She phoned the local newspaper no less than seven times chasing Denise's friend and finally cornered him in the butcher's at lunchtime on Thursday.

One of the advantages of living in a small community—you could run, but not for long, and you sure as hell couldn't hide. She promised him a good show and he promised her a reporter. She left in high spirits.

Quinn had been as good as his word and e-mailed her a precisely written statement to read during the meeting. It cited precedents and bylaws and subsections and clauses. She couldn't follow most of it, but she figured that probably meant that the majority of the councillors wouldn't be able to, either, which was good. She wanted them to be intimidated. She wanted them to know they were going to have a fight on their hands if they tried to push this thing through.

Her great-grandfather had built the Grand in 1929. He'd commissioned an architect in Sydney and imported marble from Carrara and light fittings from Venice. He'd created a wonderful legacy for the community. No way was Amy going to roll over while some greedy developer turned it to dust and replaced it with a bunch of shoe-box-size apartments.

She dressed carefully for the big meeting. A borrowed suit from Denise, neat and black and businesslike. A pair of new shoes that hurt her toes but gave her an extra four inches in height—very necessary since she was only five feet tall and often mistaken for a kid. She pulled her shoulder-length curly blond hair into a bun and painted her face with more makeup than she usually wore. She didn't want anyone mistaking her for a kid tonight.

It was only a short drive to the council chambers. Amy's new shoes pinched her feet as she walked across the gravel parking lot toward the front entrance. By the end of the evening she doubted she'd be able to feel her pinky toes, but if she won the Grand, she figured it would be well worth the sacrifice of two small digits.

She saw her family and friends the moment she walked into the meeting room. The public gallery was full of familiar faces—her parents, the Joneses, Denise,

Maria, Katherine. Cheryl and Eric from work, a few of the customers from her parents' store.

A better turnout than she'd hoped for. Which was good, right?

She made her way to the front row where tables were provided for members of the public who wanted to make notes or present evidence. She put down her bag and took a deep breath. So far, so good.

Then she looked up and saw Barry Ulrich standing with his lawyer, a young guy in a slick suit. They were talking to Reg Hanover and a couple of the other councillors, and everyone was smiling and nodding as though they were in complete and utter agreement with each other.

Amy could feel the blood drain out of her face.

Barry had brought his lawyer. And all she had was a statement from Quinn and her own very inexpert understanding of the council bylaws. She pressed a hand to her stomach. If she messed this up, it was over. The Grand would be smashed to pieces. There was no coming back from that.

Barry glanced over and caught her eye. His smile broadened and he gave her a friendly little wave. As though this was a cocktail party, and he the host.

Goddamn.

She should have hired a lawyer. She'd resisted because of the expense, but it was stupid to economize when failing at this hurdle meant the end of the game. What had she been thinking with her puny little statement and her cheering squad?

"Sorry I'm late," a deep, familiar voice said from behind her. "My flight was delayed, and there was construction on the freeway."

A shiny black leather briefcase landed on the table.

Amy turned and blinked at the tall, dark-haired, dark-eyed man standing beside her.

"Quinn," she said. "You came."

CHAPTER TWO

"L<small>IKE</small> I <small>SAID</small>, I would have been here sooner but shit happened."

It had been a close-run thing, but he'd made it. And in the nick of time.

Quinn pulled a file and a legal pad from his briefcase then clicked it shut again. Only when he was satisfied that he was ready to roll did he look Amy fully in the face.

Her blond curls had been tamed into a conservative bun, and her face was less full and her cheekbones more prominent than when he'd last seen her. His gaze got caught for a moment on her lower lip, full and shiny with gloss, then slid lower to take in her neat little suit and towering high heels.

He frowned.

"You look different." He wasn't sure if he liked it. Whenever he pictured Amy in his mind's eye, her hair was always wild and her clothes mismatched. Most importantly, she was always laughing. The woman standing in front of him looked as though she'd had all the laughter drained out of her.

"Do I?"

"Yeah. Since when did you start wearing suits?"

"Since I borrowed this from Denise." She shook her head. "I can't believe you're really here."

"I did a bit of checking into Ulrich," he said. "Guy's got some serious connections around town. Figured you might need someone to ride shotgun."

Her gaze searched his face just as his had searched hers. He wondered if he looked as tired as he felt, if she could see past the mask he'd worn for months now.

Before either of them could say any more, a middle-aged man wearing the ugliest tie he'd ever seen banged a wooden gavel on the long table placed before the council members.

"This council meeting is now in session. I call upon the secretary, Councillor McMahon, to read over the minutes from the previous meeting."

A gray-haired woman with a severely short haircut began to drone her way through the minutes. Quinn turned to Amy but she spoke before he could get the question out of his mouth.

"Reg Hanover," she said. "He's the chairman, and Dulcie McMahon is the one speaking."

Quinn drew a quick representation of the council table on his notepad and labeled the central position and the secretary. Amy reached across and slid his pen from his hand, an old trick of hers from high school. She angled his notepad toward herself and started jotting names in the other six seats along the table, indicating official roles where applicable. He glanced at her profile as she wrote. She might have swapped her usual bright, haphazard fashion for a suit and high heels, but she still poked the tip of her tongue between her lips when she was concentrating.

He suppressed a smile.

She glanced up at him and quirked an eyebrow. *What?*

He shrugged. *Nothing.*

She pushed his notepad toward him.

"What happened to Hamilton Island?" she asked quietly, one eye on the councillors.

"It'll keep. I wanted to make sure you were over the line first."

A flurry of yays drew his attention to the front of the room as the councillors voted to accept the minutes as a true record of the last meeting.

Quinn could feel someone watching him and he glanced to his left to find a man in his midfifties scowling at him. Ulrich, if Quinn didn't miss his guess. The older man had the flushed complexion of a heavy drinker and his pale blond hair was brushed carefully to try to disguise the fact that it was thinning.

Quinn held the man's gaze for a few long seconds. Ulrich's scowl deepened, then he looked away.

It was enough to tell Quinn that the guy was a hothead. Which meant this meeting had the potential to get interesting. Quinn smiled slightly as he returned his attention to the front of the room. He'd never been afraid of a fight.

Amy sat straighter as the chairman cleared his throat.

"First up on the agenda is the sale of the Grand Picture Theatre to Ulrich Construction. All councillors have received copies of a proposal from Ulrich Construction to redevelop the property into an apartment building offering luxury accommodation for tourists visiting the area," the chairman said.

He shuffled the papers in front of him then glanced quickly around the room—avoiding looking directly at Amy, Quinn noted. Guilty little rat.

Reg went on to read from the most flowery sections of Ulrich's proposal, effectively selling the project on the other man's behalf. Not hard to work out which side Hanover thought his bread was buttered on.

Amy's hands tightened on her pen until her knuckles were white. He leaned closer to her ear. "We're not leaving until the Grand is safe. I promise."

He could smell her perfume, something sweet and light. One of her curls had escaped her bun to brush her cheek. She nodded her understanding but retained her death grip on the pen. He understood her fear. He doubted she'd be able to relax until after this meeting was over.

"Council has reviewed the proposal and considers it to be of benefit to the greater community of Daylesford," the chairman said. "However, in accordance with policy, we now invite any members of the public who may wish to comment to take the floor."

His words were still echoing around the chamber as Amy stood, her chair scraping across the floor.

"I have a few questions for council," she said. There was a nervous quaver in her voice, but her chin was high and her shoulders square. "I'd like to know what measures the council has in place to ensure that Ulrich Construction's development will preserve the unique architectural features of the Grand Picture Theatre. Features which are detailed in the town's own historical register."

"I'm not conversant with the exact wording of the register, Amy, but what you must understand is—"

"I have copies," Amy said, holding up a handful of photocopies.

A woman with garnet-red hair popped up from her seat in the front of the public gallery. She winked at Quinn as she crossed the room and took the copies from Amy. It took him a moment to realize it was Denise Jenkins. She'd had mousy brown hair when he'd last seen her.

"Thanks, 'Nise," Amy whispered.

"Kick ass, sweetie," Denise whispered back. Then she turned to distribute the copies to the council members.

"I have a copy for you, too, Mr. Ulrich, in case you aren't aware that both the interior and exterior of the theatre are listed for protection," Amy said.

She held a sheet out, but both Ulrich and his lawyer ignored her. Surprise, surprise. The last thing they wanted was to hear about the architectural features they planned to turn to rubble at the earliest opportunity.

Amy shrugged, then launched into her argument. She was passionate and articulate, her small body vibrating with determination. Quinn alternated between making notes and watching her face. Despite the circumstances, despite the distance that had grown between them, it was good to see her. To look into her familiar brown eyes and hear her voice.

Opening salvo fired, Amy sat. She glanced at him and he smiled. She offered him a nervous grimace in return.

Ulrich's lawyer stood next, launching into a soliloquy on the "extraordinary and prohibitively expensive" accommodations Ulrich had built into his plans to preserve the theatre's historic facade, painting the other man as a community benefactor sacrificing personal wealth for the good of all.

"What a load of bullshit," Amy muttered under her breath.

"Come on, the guy's clearly a saint," Quinn murmured. "One step away from being recognized by the Pope."

"Thank you, Mr. Collins," Reg said when the lawyer was done. "I think we've all heard enough to make an informed decision. Ladies and gentlemen, I believe we're ready to vote."

Quinn almost laughed at the clumsiness of the other man's tactics. They'd barely opened discussion, yet the chairman was trying to ram the vote through. Quinn was suddenly very, very glad that he'd decided to ditch his vacation.

An angry murmur went up from the gallery. Amy started to stand again, but he caught her arm.

"My turn, I think," he said quietly.

He rose. "Before you start tallying votes, Chairman Hanover, I'd like to draw the council's attention to a number of recent findings in the Victorian Supreme Court. It might be helpful for council to understand what penalties have been applied to cases where historically listed sites have been exploited by unscrupulous developers."

That brought Ulrich's lawyer to his feet.

"I object to the inference that my client is unscrupulous," the younger man said.

"Go right ahead. But you might want to remember that we're not in a court of law so there's no one to actually uphold your objection," Quinn said. "But please, feel free if it increases your billable hours."

Ulrich's lawyer turned a dull brick-red. Quinn refocused on the council members. Eight men and women, all of them looking decidedly uncomfortable. They were about to get more so.

"I'd also like to remind councillors that when they were elected to office they took an oath which binds them to a code of conduct which requires them to uphold all the bylaws of the county, not simply those which are deemed convenient at the time."

Several of the councillors shifted in their seats. Quinn undid the button on his jacket and slid his hands into his trouser pockets. He had the floor, and he wasn't giving it up until he had these bastards on the run.

"Where was I? Right, the State of Victoria versus Simpkin-Gist Construction…"

TWO HOURS LATER, Amy exited the council building and stopped on the front steps to suck in big lungfuls of cool night air. She was a little light-headed after the tension of the past few hours. Her armpits were damp with sweat, she'd chewed her thumbnail down to the quick, and she didn't know whether to laugh or cry or jump with joy.

She owned the Grand. As of fifteen minutes ago, Quinn had talked the council into signing the sale contract. She'd had to pay more than she'd anticipated, thanks to Ulrich upping the ante, but it was hers. At last. After ten years and a last-minute rush to the finish line.

If didn't feel quite real.

"Here you are! One minute you were standing there, surrounded by everyone, the next you were gone," her mother said from behind her.

Amy turned to face her. "I needed some fresh air. It all got a bit crazy in there once the contract was finalized."

The doors opened behind them and her father and Quinn joined them, both smiling broadly.

"I was just telling Quinn that I haven't enjoyed anything so much since Mohammed Ali took on George Foreman in the Rumble in the Jungle. The way he took those councillors apart…" Her father clapped a hand onto Quinn's shoulder and gave him an approving shake.

"It was a pleasure, believe me," Quinn said.

Amy looked at him, standing there with his dark hair gleaming in the light from the street lamp. He'd been her knight in shining armor tonight, riding up out of nowhere and vanquishing her enemies. Her heart swelled with old, foolish emotions.

"Quinn, I don't know what to say. You gave up your holiday—Lisa is probably cursing my name—and you won me the Grand."

Even though she knew it probably wasn't the smartest thing to do given her unrequited crush, Amy stepped forward and pressed a kiss to his cheek.

"Thank you! From the bottom of my heart."

She started to pull away but Quinn's arms came around her and the next thing she knew she was clamped against his chest and he was spinning her around.

"You made it, Ames," he said. "Woohoo!"

His wool coat was as soft as silk beneath her hands, his body beneath it big and strong. She closed her eyes and inhaled the smell of expensive fabric and subtle, woody aftershave.

"And it only took ten years and every cent she's ever earned," her father said drily.

Quinn set her on her feet and she tried to look as though her heart wasn't pounding out of control because he'd held her in his arms for a few short seconds.

"We need to celebrate," she said. "We need to drink champagne and thank the gods that Quinn decided to become a lawyer instead of a doctor when he applied to university all those years ago."

Her father looked rueful. "I'd love to, sweetheart, but we've got that lumber shipment coming in first thing. If I have a glass of wine now I'll be useless tomorrow."

This was true, Amy knew. For a big, shambling bear of a man, her father was a very cheap drunk.

"Maybe we can do something tomorrow night, then." She glanced at Quinn. "How long are you in town?"

"The weekend. But you can't go home and put on your jim-jams after a win like this. If your folks are going to wimp out, I'll take you out."

Her mother pretended to be offended as she gave Quinn a push on the arm.

"You watch yourself, Quinn Whitfield. Your mother and I still e-mail regularly. I can get you into big trouble if I want to."

"My humble apologies, Mrs. P. I stand corrected."

Amy fumbled in her bag for her notepad.

"That reminds me. I promised Louise I'd let her know what happened tonight," Amy said. She added a note to e-mail Quinn's mom with her news to her To Do list. Quinn's parents had been on the road in their RV since his father retired last year, their house empty and silent next door, but like her mother, Amy kept up contact via e-mail.

When she glanced up from writing her note, Quinn was watching her with amused eyes.

"What's with the notepad?" he asked.

"It helps me stay organized."

He raised an eyebrow.

"It does!" she insisted.

"It's true, Quinn. Amy is the best paint department manager we've ever had at the store, thanks to that little pad," her mother said.

"Guess we're going to lose her now, though, huh?" her father said.

Amy smiled fondly at her parents. They had never ceased to support her, even though she knew there were probably times when they'd been convinced she'd never achieve her dream. She put her arm around her father's waist and gave him a little squeeze. He dropped a kiss onto the top of her head, his eyes suspiciously shiny. After a few seconds, he cleared his throat.

"Well, I guess we'll leave you kids to it."

Her parents headed home and Quinn took her elbow and started steering her toward a nondescript sedan parked at the far corner of the parking lot.

"Hey. I need my car," she said.

"Not tonight. Tonight you're going to drink champagne and kick up your heels and get messy drunk," Quinn said.

She glanced at his profile as they walked, his features barely visible in the dark. Despite all the reasons why it should be wrong, it felt right that Quinn was here to celebrate with her.

She smirked as Quinn cut in front of her to open her car door for her.

"So courtly, Mr. Whitfield," she said. "So sophisticated."

He gave her a dry look. "I know you're probably used to being thrown into the back of a truck or over a shoulder, but up in the big smoke we're a little smoother."

"Do tell," she said, fluttering her eyelashes at him as she slid into the car.

He pushed the door closed and circled to the driver's side.

"You know what we should do? Bribe Phil into selling us a bottle of champagne and take it to the Grand," Amy said as Quinn got behind the wheel.

Phil ran the local pub and could generally be relied upon to supply a bottle of wine to desperate locals when the liquor shop was closed for the night.

Quinn pulled onto the road.

"As a member of the New South Wales Bar Association, it behooves me to inform you that purchasing alcohol from a licensed facility for consumption off premises is a crime," Quinn said in the same tone he'd used to destroy Reg Hanover and Barry Ulrich earlier in the evening.

"So you want me to run in and get it, then?"

"Nah. It'll be good to catch up with Phil," Quinn said with a quick grin.

A rush of warm emotion washed over her. It was only now that Quinn was sitting beside her, so familiar and dear, that she was able to acknowledge how much she'd missed him. How painful her self-imposed isolation had been. His laugh, his dry sense of humor, his honesty, his patience and kindness—she'd missed him like crazy for every second of the eighteen months she'd tried to cut him out of her life.

Which went to show how effective her cold-turkey regime had been.

"Lisa must have been pretty pissed with you for canceling Hamilton Island," she said.

Good to remind herself of Lisa. Quinn's wife. Her friend. Good to always keep those two very important facts top of mind, before she got too caught up in the feelings swamping her.

There was a short silence as Quinn pulled into a parking spot outside the pub.

"The old oak's gone," he said.

She glanced at him, aware that he hadn't responded to her comment. Did that mean he was in the dog house over helping her out? She hoped not.

"It fell over in a storm last year."

"Must have been some storm."

They got out of the car and Quinn took a moment to scan the town's main thoroughfare.

She looked, too, and wondered what he saw. The heritage shopfronts, or the fact that there was only one butcher? The well-tended flower beds and handmade park benches, or the fact that the post office doubled as a news agency as well as a lottery outlet?

"I suppose it must all seem pretty tin-pot compared to the bright lights of Sydney," she said.

He met her eyes across the car.

"It's home, Ames. That's what it seems like."

His mouth tilted upward at the corner, but he looked sad. Or maybe lost. Amy frowned, suddenly remembering the long silences during their recent phone conversation.

It was on the tip of her tongue to ask if anything was wrong but Quinn turned away and started walking toward the pub.

"Phil still trying to give up smoking?" he asked.

"Every year. Last time he held out a whole month."

"Wow. That's got to be a new record, right?"

"No way. I think you're forgetting the great abstinence of '95 when he went a full three months without touching the demon nicotine."

"Right. My mistake."

Quinn was smiling again as they pushed through the double doors into the bar. She told herself she'd imagined the small moment by the car, that it had simply been a trick of the light.

And even if she hadn't imagined it, she had no right to pry into Quinn's private thoughts and feelings. Not when she'd been trying to cut him out of her life for the past year and a half.

The news of her successful purchase of the Grand had spread through town and it was twenty minutes before she'd finished accepting congratulations from her friends and acquaintances. Phil handed over a bottle of his best

French champagne but refused to accept any money for it.

"Against the liquor laws, Amy," he said with a wink at Quinn. "Plus I figure I'll hit you up for some free movie tickets when you've got the old girl up and running again."

"You're on," Amy said.

He loaned them a couple of champagne flutes and she and Quinn left the pub and began walking up Vincent Street to where the roofline of the Grand soared over its neighbors.

By mutual unspoken consent, their steps slowed as they approached and they craned their necks to take in the faded grandeur of the facade.

"I'd forgotten how imposing it is. It really is grand, isn't it?" Quinn said.

"Yep," she said around the lump in her throat.

She sniffed as quietly as she could and blinked rapidly.

She could feel Quinn looking at her and she turned her head away slightly, trying to mask her tears.

"You crying, Ames?"

"Yep."

Quinn's laughter sounded low and deep. "I think we need to get some champagne into you."

"Let's go inside first."

"You've got a key already?" He sounded surprised.

"Don't need one. The back door hasn't shut properly since the last tenant moved out."

"Our second crime for the evening—breaking and entering. I'm starting to feel like Bonnie and Clyde. We're on a rampage."

She started up the alley that led to the parking lot at the rear of the cinema.

"Technically, it's only entering, since the door is already screwed," she said.

"Those are the little details that make all the difference in court."

"If you're afraid, Whitfield, you can wait outside."

"Nice try, Parker, but I'm not letting you swill all the champagne on your own. I've developed a taste for the finer things in life over the past few years, in case you hadn't noticed."

"City slicker."

"Yokel."

They'd reached the back of the theatre and she dropped her shoulder against the decrepit door, trying to shove it open.

"For Pete's sake. You weight less than a gnat. Let me do it," Quinn said. He stepped forward.

"I've got it," she said.

"Amy…"

She took a step back and threw her entire body weight at the door. It gave instantly and she stumbled over the threshold.

"Break anything?" he asked as she rubbed her shoulder with her free hand.

"No. You? Your precious male ego permanently dented because you didn't get a chance to show off how much stronger you are than me?"

It was very dark in the corridor. Quinn's laugh sounded loud in the small space.

"Small of stature, big of attitude. Same old, same old."

She jumped when his hand landed on her shoulder.

"Lead the way, bossy pants," he said. "I'm at your mercy."

"I've got a flashlight in my bag…" she said, very aware of the weight and warmth of his hand on her shoulder.

She inhaled his aftershave again as she fumbled in her

handbag. He'd felt so big and solid when he'd lifted her earlier. Bigger than she remembered.

Her fumbling hand closed around the flashlight and she pulled it from her handbag and flicked it on.

"See? All good."

She felt shaky inside, as though all her internal organs were trembling. This was why she'd tried to cut him out of her life. One look, one touch and she was thinking about all the things that she'd never have. It was too hard. Too cruel. Too crazy-making.

And way, way too frustrating.

As she'd hoped, Quinn's hand fell to his side. She turned and started picking her way up the corridor. The flashlight beam bounced along the floor in front of her. A door loomed ahead and she twisted the handle and pushed it open. They emerged into a large, open space. In the old days, the screen would have filled the wall to the right of the door and the main seating would be in front of them. Now there was just a blank wall and lots of space where the seats used to be. She swung the flashlight in a wide arc, the beam glancing off scarred floors, scratched wood paneling, crumbling plaster walls.

"Whoa. It smells in here," Quinn said.

"The roof leaked a while back. It took council a while to approve the expenditure to get it fixed and the carpet in the balcony section rotted."

Quinn gestured for her to hand over the champagne bottle and she held the beam steady while he removed the cage and popped the cork. He drew a champagne flute from his coat pocket and poured a glass, handing it over to her before repeating the process for himself.

"To the Grand," Quinn said.

She lifted her glass to his. The small clink of glass on glass was swallowed by the vastness of the space.

"Thank you for being here when I needed you," she said. "You're a good friend, Quinn."

Suddenly they were both very serious. They stared into each other's eyes for a long moment. She knew what he was thinking about—those eighteen months of unreturned phone calls and e-mails. Guilt and longing twisted inside her. She turned away and took a big gulp of champagne. Bubbles tickled the back of her throat and she coughed.

"Careful there, tiger," he said.

She walked away from him, playing the flashlight over the nearest wall.

"Do you know they imported all the cherrywood for this paneling from Northern California, even though they could have used local lacewood or blackwood? My great-grandfather was so obsessed with creating a masterpiece he wanted everything in this place to be exotic and expensive," she said.

Quinn joined her, reaching out to run a hand along one of the panels.

"It's pretty scratched up."

"Years of neglect and indifference will do that."

"Can I?" he asked, indicating the flashlight.

"Sure." She handed it over and leaned against the wall as he took a tour of the theatre. She watched him pass the light over the piles of debris covering the floor, the remnants of past tenants, then pause to inspect the dark holes in the floors where bolts once fixed the sectional seating in place.

"Most of the seats are stored in the basement, but some of them were sold off," she said. "I've been collecting them from yard sales for the past few years, storing them at my place and in the garage at Mom and Dad's."

"Bet your dad loves that."

"He doesn't mind."

He studied the far wall before aiming the beam at the once-spectacular figured plaster ceiling. In its heyday, it had been a stylized depiction of the universe, complete with sun and moon, planets and stars. She didn't need to look up to know what he was seeing now. Mold. Crumbling plaster. Water damage.

She had a lot of hard work ahead of her, but she'd never been afraid of hard work. In fact, she welcomed it.

She sipped her champagne as Quinn circled his way back to her.

"Lot to do here, Ames."

"I know."

"Going to cost a bomb."

She shrugged. "That's what loans are for, right?" She had a detailed business plan. She'd done her homework. Once she was up and running, she was confident she'd attract enough tourist dollars to more than pay back her debts.

He drank some champagne. "So, who comes in first? Painters? Carpenters? Have you had the place surveyed?"

"It's structurally sound. The roof needs some work. New guttering, that kind of thing. I've spoken to Neville Wallace about that. He's going to fix the plumbing, too. But I'll have to retile the bathrooms myself. And paint in here, too, I guess."

She arched her neck and considered the thirty-foot-high walls. She needed to make a note to call the scaffolding company.

"You're kidding. Right?"

She looked at Quinn. He was frowning.

"I wish I was, but I just spent my painting budget. Where do you think that extra twenty thousand came from at the last minute?" She'd only hesitated for a second when Reg had upped the price by twenty thousand, hoping to scare her off and buy his buddy Ulrich more time. She'd known she'd never get another chance at the Grand if she allowed Ulrich the time to regroup and find some sneaky way around the legal arguments Quinn had put forward.

"But Amy…" Quinn shook his head, lost for speech. "This place is *huge*."

"So it's going to take a little more time than I originally planned. I can live with that."

"Do you have any idea what you're taking on?"

"Of course I do."

"How are you going to tackle the ceiling? That plaster work is part of the heritage listing."

"Thank you, Quinn. I'm aware of that, as a matter of fact. I'm aware of every inch of this place, having spent the past ten years working toward this moment. Which is why I traveled into Melbourne two nights a week to attend a course on restoring vintage decorative plasterwork last year. And why I did an upholstery course the year before that, and why I have a file a foot thick with information on suppliers who can help me refit this place."

The frown didn't leave his face. He slid his glass onto the wide lip at the top of the timber paneling.

"Amy, it's one thing to be passionate, but this place needs more than passion."

"I can handle it," she said through gritted teeth. She put down her own glass. Since when had Quinn been such a killjoy? She couldn't believe he was attacking her dream like this, trying to pull it apart before she'd even gotten used to the idea that the Grand was hers.

"I think you should get an expert restorer to take a look at—"

"Quinn, shut up."

"Amy—"

"I mean it. Don't say another word, okay, or I'm going to get really angry," she said. "I appreciate your help tonight, but I don't appreciate being patronized by someone who has no idea what they're talking about."

"I'm simply pointing out that sometimes having a dream isn't enough. Just because you want something badly doesn't mean you're going to get it. Believe me, life doesn't work like that."

There was a hard, cold edge to his voice. Once, a long time ago, he'd lain in the tall grass at the end of her parents' yard and dreamed with her. Obviously, those days were gone.

"This is the best night of my life," she said, her voice low and controlled. "I've wanted to buy this place ever since my grandfather brought me here when I was four years old and we sat up there in the balcony and he told me how his father built this place and how sad he'd been when he was forced to sell it. I am not going to stand here and listen to you tell me what I can't do and what I don't know."

She bent and grabbed the champagne bottle from the floor.

"I'll be at the pub if you want to celebrate."

"Amy."

She ignored him and strode toward the rear exit. He had the flashlight, he'd be able to find his own way out.

CHAPTER THREE

QUINN SWORE under his breath and went after her. He caught her just as she pulled open the door to the rear corridor. He reached over her head and pushed the door shut, the sound echoing sharply in the empty theatre.

"Quinn—" She tried to pull the door open but he didn't budge.

"I'm sorry, okay? I was out of line."

She looked at him, her big brown eyes decidedly cool. She was waiting for more. An explanation. He dropped his arm and took a step backward.

He had no idea what to tell her. He'd walked in here feeling proud and happy and triumphant for her. Then he'd seen how much work she'd taken on and all he could see were the pitfalls and disappointments lying in wait for her. Amy was smart and resourceful, but she'd always been an incurable optimist. She didn't understand that sometimes it didn't matter what you did or how much you tried, some things couldn't be fixed.

He opened his mouth to try to explain, to try to make her see that she needed to be more realistic, to brace herself for disappointment so she wouldn't be hurt when it arrived.

"Lisa and I are getting a divorce," he said.

Jesus, where the hell had that come from?

And since when did his voice sound like it belonged

to a twelve-year-old on the brink of sooking like a big baby?

Amy stared at him for a long, silent moment.

"But…" She blinked. "How? I don't understand…."

"Lisa met someone else."

She shook her head, her eyes wide. "No. She would never do that to you."

He smiled grimly. "As much as my ego would love to agree with you, the facts are pretty undeniable. She met him at work. He's another lawyer, a barrister. They'd been seeing each other behind my back for nearly two years when she left me."

She mouthed a four-letter word.

"There was plenty of that going on, from what I gather," he said.

"But you guys were so good together. You had so much in common."

He didn't even know how to begin explaining the failure of his marriage. The distance that had grown between him and Lisa, the anger. The dissatisfaction and arguments. He didn't fully understand it himself. He'd known they weren't happy, but he hadn't comprehended the lengths Lisa was prepared to go to to try to recapture her happiness. Without him.

"My God, Quinn, I'm so sorry."

Suddenly her arms were around him, her cheek pressed to his chest. Her palms flattened against his back as she held him close.

"I'm so sorry."

For a moment he stood very still. It had been a long time since anyone had held him this way. He'd had lovers in the year since Lisa had left, but no one had held him like they cared. Like they loved him. Like he mattered.

He wrapped his arms around Amy and rested his cheek on the crown of her head.

"Ames. God…" His voice was thick with emotion. He sucked in a ragged breath, fighting for control. He'd thought he had all this stuff under control. He'd thought he was almost over it.

Amy's fingers dug into his back as she pulled him even closer. He inhaled the sweet smell of her shampoo and absorbed the warmth of her small, strong body against his. It had been too long. He'd missed her. He hadn't realized how much until this minute. She'd always been his sounding board, his cheering squad, his devil's advocate and faithful sidekick. No wonder he'd been thinking about her so much lately. No wonder she'd been in his dreams.

Their hug lasted a long time. Slowly he got himself under control. Amy stirred and he forced himself to let her go.

"Sorry," he said. He couldn't quite meet her eyes. Talk about spilling his guts.

"I don't know what the official ruling is, but I think you're allowed to be upset when your marriage ends."

He shrugged a shoulder. "It's been eleven months. I should be over it."

"It takes as long as it takes, right?"

He shrugged again. This was all new territory for him.

She passed him the champagne bottle. He took it, grateful for the distraction. Champagne fizzed in the back of his throat as he swallowed a big mouthful straight from the bottle. He could feel Amy watching him. Now that the intensity of the initial moment had passed he felt foolish, self-conscious.

"Don't worry. I'm not about to blubber all over you," he said.

She held out a hand for the bottle and he passed it over. She took a healthy swig, then wiped her mouth with the back of her hand. Then she leveled a finger at him.

"You make one more crack about being emotional and I'm going to punch you in the face. Got it?"

He smiled. Couldn't help himself. She looked so stern with her finger aimed at him and her brown eyes so serious. She probably would try to hit him, too.

"I mean it, Quinn. Don't you dare try to pull that he-man crap with me."

He held his hands up in surrender. "Okay. Sorry. It won't happen again."

"What is it with men? When did being human become a crime? It's so *dumb*."

He figured she didn't expect him to respond. He gestured toward the main seating area with the flashlight. "You want to try this again? Only this time I'll shut the hell up."

"Don't make promises you can't keep."

He pulled the bottle from her hands and gave her a little shove on the shoulder. "Come on, give me a proper tour. Please?"

She was silent for a moment, watching him. Trying to decide if she should push him to talk more, no doubt.

A few years ago, she wouldn't have hesitated. She would have bullied him until he told her everything she wanted to know.

She smiled. "Prepare to be bored, Whitfield," she said as she headed off into the darkness. "Try to keep up."

LISA AND QUINN *are getting a divorce.*

The thought was still reverberating in Amy's mind when she crawled into bed two hours later. She and

Quinn had returned to the pub after she'd given him the tour. They'd run into a few people they'd both gone to school with, shared some bar snacks and more champagne. And all the while Amy had been trying to come to grips with Quinn's bombshell.

Now she stared at the ceiling in her bedroom. She felt as though someone had pulled the rug out from beneath her feet.

Lisa and Quinn had been teen sweethearts. They'd moved to Sydney to study law together. They'd loved each other. Their future was all mapped out.

And now it was all over. Lisa had had an affair, broken Quinn's trust.

Goddamn.

Amy simply couldn't get her head around it. Quinn was so loyal and loving. It made her chest tight to think of how betrayed he must feel. How disappointed and hurt and angry. There was no way he'd made his marriage vows six years ago expecting them to have such a limited lifespan. No. Way.

She thought back to the night before the wedding, to the things he'd said to her down on the dock at the lake. They'd both had enough drink to be feeling no pain. Quinn had been sitting opposite her leaning against a pylon, his long legs bent at the knees, his bare feet planted on the deck.

"I'VE BEEN THINKING about this for a long time," he said as he looked out over the dark water. "Getting married. Buying a place of our own. Starting a family."

She smiled, even though her grip tightened on her beer bottle. "Always were a big planner, Whitfield."

He shook his head. "I don't have it all mapped out. I

know stuff will go wrong. But I also know we'll make it work. Because we love each other, and we know each other."

She nodded. Mostly because she didn't trust herself to speak.

"What about you, Ames?" he asked suddenly, nudging her bare foot with his. "You think Aaron's going to pop the question?"

She'd been going out with Aaron Reid for over a year.

"I don't want to get married yet. I've got the Grand to think about first."

"You can get married and still restore the Grand."

"I'm not ready yet."

"You've missed your big opportunity, you know. We could have had a double wedding if you'd played your cards right."

"Aaron and I aren't like you and Lisa," she said. It came out more sharply than she'd intended and Quinn took a pull on his beer before responding.

"I just want you to be as happy as I am, Ames."

"I know. Sorry."

He shifted one of his feet so it rested on hers, big and warm, letting her know without words that she was forgiven. He smiled at her, his eyes heavy-lidded from all the alcohol.

"Tomorrow's going to be a great day. The best day of my life," he said.

Her heart ached with sadness and happiness as she looked at him, the two emotions so hopelessly mixed she knew she'd never get them untangled.

"You're going to be a great husband."

"I know," he said. Then they both laughed at his shameless arrogance.

SHE TWISTED in bed, rolling over onto her side. God, how she hated the idea that he was in pain, that all that hope and happiness had gone up in flames. Worse, that she hadn't been around to comfort him because she'd chosen to push him out of her life when he'd needed her the most.

How could Lisa have done this to him? Amy could still remember the way her friend had glowed on the morning of their wedding. And the way Quinn had looked at Lisa when she'd walked up the aisle toward him. A match made in heaven, everyone had said.

And Lisa had thrown all that away. Amy simply couldn't comprehend it.

She was drifting toward sleep when an insidious little thought weaseled its way into her mind: now that Quinn was getting a divorce, he was free again. Available.

Her eyes snapped open. Her heart kicked out an urgent, panicky beat.

Don't. Don't even think it. Not for a second, you idiot.

But she was wide-awake, and the thought was lodged in her brain, glowing like neon.

Quinn was free to love again. If he wanted to.

"Don't be an idiot," she said out loud.

Because she'd been waiting for Quinn Whitfield to notice her since she was fourteen years old. A full sixteen years of yearning, longing, jealousy and heartache. Long enough to know better.

She closed her eyes and pushed the weasel words down into a deep, dark corner of her mind. Because she *did* know better. Even if some aberrant, hope-springs-eternal, deluded part of her psyche refused to lay down and die, most of her knew the truth: Quinn had never seen her as anything other than his good friend. And nothing she ever did would change that.

SHE SLEPT BADLY and woke early. Her first thought was that Quinn was getting a divorce, her second that she now owned the Grand.

Great priorities. Not.

She lay in bed reviewing the evening's momentous events, then started to formulate plans for the day ahead. The way she saw it, she had two options—hunt down Quinn and ask all the questions she hadn't asked last night, or find Reg Hanover and talk him into giving her early access to the Grand.

She chose option B, because she might be a hopeless case where Quinn was concerned, but she wasn't stupid. No matter how wonderful and sad and torturous it was to have him in town, tomorrow he would fly home to Sydney. The Grand was her future, her big dream come true. She needed to keep that fact top of mind no matter what other distractions were on hand.

By nine she was waiting out at the front of the council building, keeping watch for Reg's distinctive beige Volvo. She saw him turn in to the parking lot and waited until he'd parked before walking toward him.

"Ms. Parker," he said stiffly as he exited her car. "To what do I owe this pleasure?"

Amy spared a glance for today's tie—a sketchily drawn blue marlin leaping on a purple background— before focusing on Reg's face.

"I want to talk to you about getting access to the Grand before settlement."

"I'm afraid that's not possible." His tone implied that he thought her request was inappropriate, to say the least.

Amy gave him her brightest smile. "I don't see why not. It happens all the time, and it's not as though there's a tenant. The place has been empty for years. Surely it's to the community's benefit that the restoration start as soon as possible?"

Reg opened his mouth to reject her again.

"Before you say no, I should warn you that I'll be back tomorrow to ask the same thing. And the day after that, and so on. I've always been stubborn like that."

"Tomorrow's Sunday."

"I know, but I also know where you live, Reg."

He glared at her, his thick eyebrows meeting in the middle. She could see his desire to punish her for last night's defeat warring with his need to be rid of her. She held her breath, waiting to see which way he would jump.

Ten minutes later she was pushing the chrome-and-glass front doors of the Grand wide open. She stepped into the dusty foyer and glanced around.

"Honey, I'm home," she called, her voice echoing in the empty space.

It was tempting to gloat a little, but she'd done her celebrating last night. She rolled up the sleeves on her bright orange sweater and performed her first act as owner of the Grand, tearing down the tattered yellow paper that had masked the front windows for years. Light streamed into the foyer, unkindly highlighting the old cinema's many flaws.

"Don't worry, baby. We'll put you right."

An hour later she was dragging a small mountain of damp cardboard out to the rear parking lot. She'd arranged for an industrial-size rubbish bin to be delivered first thing Monday, but she was too impatient to wait until then to get started. She hefted the cardboard onto the pile she'd created near the door just as a dark sedan pulled up next to her rusty old station wagon. It took her a moment to recognize Quinn behind the wheel. She dusted her hands down the front of her jeans as he exited his car.

"I should have known you'd be here," he said.

He was wearing faded jeans and scuffed brown boots with a charcoal-gray sweater. Her heart did stupid, teen-age things as she took in his broad shoulders and lean hips and wry smile.

"No point in wasting time."

"How much rent are the council charging you to have early access?"

"None."

He lifted an eyebrow. "How'd you pull that off?"

"I have my ways," she said mysteriously.

He looked amused. "Sure you do. You want a hand?"

He'd caught her off guard. "It's nice of you to offer, but it's mostly donkey work. Clearing out all the crap the old tenants have left behind."

"I'm not afraid of hard work."

"Yeah, but I don't want to chew up all your time. You're only home for the weekend."

Plus I'm a little out of practice putting on my game face when you're around. Witness the fact that I've got goose bumps just because you're standing a few feet away, smiling at me.

"I came home to help you, Ames. I'm all yours for the weekend." He walked past her toward the entrance. "Want to show me what needs doing?"

He disappeared inside the building. She stared after him, thrown.

It's no big deal, Parker. A few hours aren't going to

kill you. It's not like you're going to suddenly jump on him after sixteen years of self-restraint.

Sliding her hands into her back pockets, she followed him into the corridor.

The power wouldn't be connected until Monday, but there was enough light filtering through the archway to the foyer and the propped-open back door to see what they were up against. She gestured toward the moldering piles of carpet, tattered cartons, broken furniture and other flotsam and jetsam littering the floor. The worst of it had been masked by the shadows last night, but now it was revealed for what it was: a lot of backbreaking work.

"Like I said, it's mostly donkey work."

He surveyed the space with his hands on his hips. Then he glanced at her. "You realize you're going to owe me dinner after this, right?"

"How does McDonald's sound?"

"Inadequate."

"I'll see what else I can come up with."

Quinn gave her a dry look before reaching for the waistband of his sweater and pulling it over his head. He was wearing a plain white T-shirt underneath, the soft fabric molding his shoulders and chest and belly. She deliberately looked away.

Nothing to see here. Please move on.

"Let's get this party started, city boy," she said.

It had been a long time since Quinn had used his muscles for anything except lifting weights at the gym. It felt good to do something real for a change. To get out of his head and lose himself in the rhythms of physical labor.

By midday they'd cleared more than half of the debris

from the main theatre and the balcony section. They walked across the road to get sandwiches for lunch and sat on the marble steps to eat, talking occasionally but mostly just eating and thinking their own thoughts.

For the first time in a long time, something inside Quinn relaxed. He felt…okay. As though he was exactly where he needed to be.

He glanced at Amy. She had a far-off look in her eyes as she gazed around the foyer while she munched on her sandwich. A faint smile curled his mouth. No doubt she was imagining the foyer as it should be. Or turning over some other notion in her mind. You never knew with Amy.

He liked that she didn't feel compelled to fill every lull with meaningless conversation. It was one of the things he'd always appreciated about her.

Lisa, on the other hand, couldn't tolerate silence. She was always the first to talk if there was a pause in the conversation. When they'd lived together the radio or stereo had always been on, music blaring to fill up the empty corners of the house. In the months before she'd left she'd progressed to leaving the TV on while they ate dinner. She'd claimed she found it comforting. Even though it had sometimes driven him nuts, he'd tolerated it because he'd wanted her to be happy.

Sitting next to Amy, he belatedly realized that his soon-to-be ex-wife had been hiding behind all that noise. Disguising her guilt and excitement over her affair, creating a buffer between them. And he'd been so busy bending over backward to please her that he hadn't noticed she'd been pulling away from him.

"You okay?" Amy asked.

"Yeah. Why?"

"You're frowning."

"No, I'm not." He made an effort to smooth his forehead.

She was silent for a beat. "Want to talk about it?"

She was sitting so close he could see the gold flecks in her eyes when she turned to look at him. He studied her long lashes, the curve of her cheek, the turned-up end of her nose. Her face was as familiar to him as his own. More so, in some ways, since he'd spent a hell of a lot more time looking at her over the years than he had looking in the mirror.

"You don't want to hear me bitch and moan."

"Wouldn't have asked if I didn't mean it."

He glanced down at his hands. "Not much to say, really."

"Are you angry?"

"Yes. Of course I am. She cheated on me for two years. Lied to me."

"Your pride's hurt. You feel humiliated." It was both a question and a statement.

He glared at her but she just cocked an eyebrow.

"Yes," he finally said.

"Do you miss her?"

He frowned, focusing on his hands again. He'd skinned his knuckles earlier and he rubbed his thumb back and forth over the raw skin.

Did he miss Lisa? The sound of her brisk footsteps on the polished floors. Her ready laughter. Her eternal restlessness and need to go one better, one better, one better.

"Not as much as I should," he said.

That shut Amy up. He glanced at her. She was picking at a worn patch on the knee of her jeans.

"Shocked you?" he asked.

"No. I guess… I always thought you and Lisa were happy. Whenever I visited, you always seemed to be. Which was why I was so surprised last night."

"We were, for a while. But Lisa always wanted more. Bigger house. Better office. Faster car."

Amy nodded. She knew Lisa almost as well as he did. She knew how ambitious Lisa had always been, how much she'd wanted to get ahead.

"And you didn't want any of that stuff?" Amy asked.

"Sure I did. Up to a point. But there are other things in life. Family. Children. Having a life, instead of spending every freaking hour at the office or at some client function, trying to drum up more business."

He could hear how resentful and angry he sounded. Amy didn't need all this crap dumped on her.

"It's okay," she said. Reading his mind, as always.

"It's done."

"No, it isn't. It's still eating you up inside."

He looked into her gold-flecked eyes again. Typical Amy, straight for the jugular, no messing around.

"Because I was dumb. That's why I can't let it go." He hadn't meant to say anything more, but the words were suddenly in his throat. "Because I should have said stop. Made us both look around and acknowledge what we were doing. But I played along way past the point when it wasn't what I wanted anymore."

"It's not your fault, Quinn."

"It's partly my fault. And now I've got this life, this job, and I have no idea…" He clamped his jaw shut and stood. "Talk about a pity party. Next I'll be asking you to braid my hair and lend me a tampon. Do me a favor and pretend the last few minutes didn't happen, okay?"

She stood, as well. "I've seen you rolling around on

the ground after being kneed in the cojones on the football field. I think I can handle a bit of existential angst."

As always, she made him laugh. He hooked his arm around her neck and pulled her close, dropping a kiss onto the top of her head. "I appreciate the ear."

"You know me, all ears." She pushed away from his chest. "We'd better get back to it."

She jumped down the last two steps to the foyer and strode through the archway into the theatre. He took his time following her.

He'd flown down to help her achieve her dream, but maybe being here was something that he needed, too. He could breathe properly here. There were no expectations, no demands. Just Amy and the comfort of home.

An idea started to form. Before he could think it to death, he followed Amy into the theatre.

"I was thinking," he said.

She turned to face him, eyebrows raised questioningly.

"I've got another week of leave after this one, and four more owing. If you want, I can hang around, help you get a good start on the restoration."

He didn't know what he'd expected, but definitely not profound silence and the blank look on her face. She looked so shocked that he laughed.

"You look like I just pulled a gun on you."

"You took me by surprise, that's all. I can't ask you to throw away your holidays helping me. You've already swooped in at the drop of a hat to save my bacon. It's too much."

"You're not asking, I'm offering. And I'd rather be here helping you out than lying on a beach somewhere swatting flies."

"You say that now, but after a few weeks of me bossing you around you'll be dreaming of a beach. Maybe we should just cut out the middleman."

He studied her face, trying to get a read on her. He'd thought she'd leap at his offer. "Afraid I'll hold it over you for the rest of our lives, Ames?"

"No. It's not that. It's…too much."

He frowned. "A few weeks' work? It's nothing."

Something flickered behind her eyes. Something he didn't understand. He'd thought they'd slotted back into their old friendship last night, but maybe he'd been wrong.

"Is there something else going on, Ames?"

"No. I think you're nuts wanting to pour all your vacation time into my white elephant. But if you want to do it, who am I to look a gift laborer in the mouth? Welcome on board."

When he didn't respond straightaway she threw her hands in the air.

"That wasn't very grateful, was it? Let me try again." She dropped to her knees and clasped her hands together in a beseeching gesture. "Thank you, Quinn Whitfield, for your generous offer above and beyond the call of duty, friendship and the Australian way. You will be remembered in the history books as a gullible but generous fool."

He couldn't help smiling at the goofy look on her face, even though his gut was still uneasy. For the first time ever with Amy he wasn't sure where he stood.

He didn't like the feeling. At all.

"Get up, you idiot."

"I think you mean *get up, boss lady.* Since you signed on to be my minion."

"In your dreams."

She stood and brushed off her knees. "I guess I'm going to owe you a lot of cheeseburgers, huh?"

She smiled at him, her expression open and uncomplicated. He looked into her big brown eyes and the edgy feeling dissolved. This was Amy, after all. If she had a problem with him, she'd come right out and say it. That was the way it had always been between them.

THE UNEASY FEELING bit him on the ass again later that day. They worked till the light faded and it was too dim to see safely. Amy insisted on sweeping the floor before they left for the day, so he volunteered to do a pizza run for dinner.

Dino's Pizza was still at the end of the block. The old neon pizza outline on the front awning had been replaced with a more aesthetically pleasing heritage-style sign, but inside the place looked the same, the small dine-in area crammed with half a dozen tables with red-and-white checked tablecloths and old raffia-wrapped chianti bottles acting as candle holders. The menu still featured his old favorites, although he noted that the fashion for all things gourmet hadn't passed Daylesford by—there were half a dozen deluxe pizzas on offer featuring such exotic ingredients as brie, artichoke hearts and smoked salmon. He ordered an old-school super supreme because he knew that was what Amy liked.

A tall blond-haired guy entered as Quinn sank onto the bench seat to wait for his order to be ready. Quinn smiled as recognition hit.

"Rick Bachelor. How are you?" he asked, standing to shake the other man's hand.

Rick grinned. "Hey. Quinn. Didn't know you were in town."

"Yeah. Came down to help Amy out," he said.

Rick had lost a bit of hair and put on a little around the middle, but otherwise he looked almost the same as he had at Quinn and Lisa's wedding six years ago.

"Right. I heard on the grapevine that Amy finally bought the Grand. Pretty impressive achievement, sticking to her guns all these years."

"Yeah. She knows what she wants, that's for sure. So, how are things?" Quinn asked.

"Great. Naomi's about to pop with our second, so we're at Def-Con four, waiting for her water to break."

"Not Naomi Wilkins?" Quinn asked, putting two and two together.

Naomi and Rick had both gone to Daylesford Secondary with him and Amy and Lisa.

"Sorry, I assumed you'd have heard. Too used to small-town gossip, I guess. I finally talked her into marrying me a couple of years ago. We've got a little girl already." Rick tugged out his wallet and Quinn found himself looking at a photograph of a little girl with big blue eyes and a very wet mouth.

"Teething," Rick explained.

"She's lovely."

"How about you and Lisa? Any kids yet?"

Quinn hesitated a moment. "No kids," he said. Then he shrugged. "Actually, we're getting a divorce."

Rick's eyes widened and Quinn could see the other man searching for something appropriate to say. It was one of the reasons Quinn hated telling people. That, and the sense of failure he felt.

"I'm sorry. That's bad news," Rick said uncomfortably.

"Yeah, well. These things happen," Quinn said.

He saw with relief that the server was trying to make eye contact with him to let him know his pizza was ready. He offered Rick his hand again.

"Looks like I'm up. Good to see you, mate."

"Likewise."

Quinn paid for his pizza and headed back to the Grand. It was well and truly twilight by now and the cars driving past had their headlights on.

It was dim inside the theatre but Amy was still busy sweeping when he entered.

"I bring pizza. Put the broom down before I'm forced to hurt you."

"I'm done. My arms feel like they're ready to fall off."

She sank onto an upturned mop bucket. Quinn pushed an old milk crate across the floor to join her and placed the pizza box on the floor between them.

"Dig in. I got your favorite, Dino's super supreme."

She took a second to respond. "Smells great."

He flipped the box open and grabbed a slice. He took a bite and gasped.

"Hot." He swallowed hastily and noticed Amy had played it smart and was waiting for her pizza to cool, letting her slice rest on her knee before she tackled it.

"Bumped into Rick Bachelor while I was waiting," he said.

"He comes into the hardware store all the time. Did he say if Naomi's had her baby yet?"

"Any day now. He said she's ready to pop."

"Did he ask about you and Lisa?"

He glanced at her, surprised. "You psychic or something?"

"Don't have to be. It's what people do. Single people get asked if they've met anyone. Unmarried couples get asked if they've set the date yet. And married couples get asked if they've got any kids. Right?"

"Yeah. That's what he asked."

"People are so nosy," she said, shaking her head.

"He was just making conversation. Being polite."

"If you want to be polite, you talk about the weather. You don't ask if people are having sex for reproductive purposes or if they're worried they're going to miss the boat."

Quinn laughed.

"I'm serious. You should hear some of the things people say to me because I'm single. 'Don't worry, someone will come along.' And my personal favorite, 'I guess that's the problem with being choosy.'"

He started to tell her she wasn't choosy, simply discerning, but he frowned as he spotted a small pile of black circles on the thigh of her jeans. It took him a moment to work out what he was looking at: olives.

She'd picked all the olives off her slice of pizza.

"You don't like olives?"

"Nope. Never have, really."

He stared at her. Somewhere, in the back of his mind, a memory stirred: a much younger Amy pulling a face and spitting out a half-chewed mouthful of food. *These round things are disgusting.* They'd both been eight, and they'd stolen a plate of hors d'oeuvres from one of his parents' dinner parties.

"So why go for the super supreme?" he asked, puzzled.

"I usually don't." She met his eyes. Which was when the penny dropped.

Super supreme was Lisa's favorite.

He groaned. "Shit. I'm sorry, Ames."

"It doesn't matter."

He stood, angry with himself for making such a stupid mistake. "Give me ten minutes, I'll go grab us another one."

"Seriously, Quinn. It's fine. I'm really not that hungry. This'll do me." She lifted the slice in her hand. The slice she'd had to quietly denude of olives before she could stomach it.

"I should have asked," he said.

"Like I said, it doesn't matter." To prove her point, she took a big bite of pizza.

He sat back down. They were both silent for the next few minutes, then Quinn pointed a finger at her. "Ham and mushroom. That's your favorite, right?"

"That's me. Ham and mushroom."

He took another piece of pizza, but his appetite had deserted him.

In the old days, there was no way Amy would have let him get away with something like that. She'd have made him go get her another pizza, then she would have held his forgetfulness over his head for the next few weeks until she'd committed some folly of her own that tipped the balance in his favor.

He'd suspected it this afternoon, and now he knew— something had shifted between them. And not in a good way.

Maybe it was to do with the divorce. Maybe she felt torn between him and Lisa. Maybe it was those eighteen months of silence. Or maybe she was angry with him for not confiding in her sooner, for withdrawing from their friendship while he dealt with the dissolution of his marriage.

He didn't care what it was. He wanted to fix it. Because there was no way he was losing Amy. She meant too much to him. She was too much a part of his life for him to take their friendship for granted.

He stared at the pockmarked floors between his bent knees for a long moment. Then he lifted his head and caught her eye.

"If I've done something wrong, Ames, I wish you'd come right out and say it."

CHAPTER FOUR

AMY LIED INSTINCTIVELY. "I don't know what you mean."

"Yeah, you do. Ever since I got here—no, since before I got here—there's been this distance between us. I know we haven't spoken for months but I hoped that once we were face-to-face things would be okay. But they're not, are they? Things are weird between us. Did I screw up? Forget your birthday? Let you down somehow? Tell me what went wrong so I can fix it."

He sounded so sincere, so wounded and confused. He thought he'd done something wrong. That she'd retreated from him as a punishment.

She shook her head. "You haven't done anything wrong."

He smiled thinly. "I might not have been around much lately, but I still know when you're lying."

He was watching her steadily, waiting. She stared at him, feeling very exposed. What did he want from her? The truth? She could imagine how he'd react to that.

It's like this, Quinn. I'm in love with you. Have been since I was fourteen years old. That's why I haven't returned your phone calls and why the idea of working with you every day for five weeks makes me want to leap for joy and bang my head against a wall at the same time.

She could almost see the dawning understanding on his face, the shock, the sadness. The pity. Could almost hear the awkward questions and explanations.

There was no way she was telling him the truth. It wouldn't get either of them anywhere. It wasn't as though he could do anything to stop her loving him. Hell, he'd married one of her best friends and it hadn't stopped her stupid, foolish heart from adoring him.

And it wasn't as though he could make himself love her. If that were possible, it would have happened years ago.

"You haven't done anything wrong," she repeated more strongly. "It's been a while, that's all."

"You're pissed with me. I know I kind of went into hiding when I found out about the affair. I know you probably felt shut out—"

"I didn't." She couldn't stand the thought that he blamed himself when she was the one who had deliberately distanced herself from him. "I had some stuff going on down here, too. I could have called you, but I let things slide, as well."

"I wondered about that."

She could feel his gaze searching her face. She didn't know what else to say to him. She didn't want to lie to him any more than she had to when he was being so honest with her.

"You know I love you, right?" he said.

He'd never said it before, but she'd always known how he felt. It amazed her how wonderful it was to hear the words, even though she knew he didn't mean it the way she wished he did.

She swallowed, hard. "I love you, too." *You have no idea how much.*

"I want things to be right between us again, Ames."

"Me, too."

"Does that mean if I buy the wrong pizza again you'll

slap me upside the head rather than eat it out of politeness?"

"Sure. If you think you can handle it."

"I can handle anything you throw my way."

"Be careful what you wish for," she said, only half joking.

He caught her hand, wrapped his fingers around it. "Anything," he said, looking into her eyes. "I mean it."

There was so much warmth and affection in his open, handsome face—and yet her heart still wanted more.

She was impossibly greedy, a willful child holding out for the whole candy shop instead of the one perfectly good bonbon on offer.

He brushed his thumb across the back of her hand one last time before letting her go.

"You want another piece?"

"Sure."

He picked the olives off a slice and handed it over.

She studied it critically. "In the spirit of recent discussions—you missed a piece, slack ass," she said.

He laughed and reached across to remove the last offending olive.

"Happy?"

"Getting there."

She watched him out of the corners of her eyes as she ate. In a mere twenty-four hours he'd managed to turn her world upside down. And—as usual—he had no idea. She was going to have to be very, very careful if she was going to keep it that way. He'd picked up on her hesitation this afternoon when he offered to stay and help her, and he'd registered her lack of reaction over the pizza, too.

The fact was, she was woefully out of practice when it came to covering up her feelings for him. All the little strategies and compensations she'd developed over the years had atrophied in eighteen months. A great example: for a few precious seconds after he'd announced he'd gotten her favorite pizza, she'd been filled with a sweet, piercing joy that he'd remembered something as small and insignificant as the fact that she loved Dino's ham and mushroom with a thin crust. She'd wanted to throw her arms around him and hold him tight.

No matter what else happens, he will always be my friend, and we will always know these things about each other, she'd thought. *I'll always know how he got the long, white scar on the top of his left foot and that peanuts make him break out in a rash, and he will always know that I'm afraid of earthworms and that I once tried to fly off the roof of the garden shed.*

They were best friends. And even though she had wanted more from him for a long time, being Quinn Whitfield's best friend was not to be sneezed at.

Then he had unveiled Dino's super supreme—Lisa's pizza, for Pete's sake.

"What time do you want me tomorrow?" Quinn asked, dragging her away from her thoughts.

"How does nine sound?"

"What time are you going to be here?"

"Eight. But you're technically on vacation."

"I usually start at six-thirty. I can handle eight."

"Six-thirty. You need to get a life," she said.

He shrugged. "I'm trying to. Why do you think I'm here?"

He finished the last of the pizza and they left the Grand together.

"I'll see you tomorrow," she said as they walked to their cars.

He waited to make sure her old rust bucket started before driving out of the lot ahead of her. She started for home, then remembered that she needed to pick up some tools from her father's garage for tomorrow. She sighed and drove past her own turnoff to her parents' street. Gravel popped beneath the tires as she parked in front of the garage.

The light was on in the kitchen. She knew her parents would expect her to come in and have a coffee and maybe dessert with them. Instead, she leaned forward and rested her forehead against the steering wheel.

Five weeks.

How in hell was she going to survive five whole weeks of intimate, cozy contact with Quinn Whitfield?

She turned her head and stared across her parents' back lawn toward the dark shape of the Whitfield house next door.

Somewhere, tucked in her mother's photo album, was a snapshot of her and Quinn sharing the same teething ring—that was how long he'd been a part of her life. Since before they could walk they'd had a preference for each other, and they'd become the boon companions of each other's childhood.

Then, over what seemed like the space of one summer, Quinn had grown from her funny, daring buddy into a startling, disturbing almost-man. He'd shot up four inches. His voice had deepened. And every time he looked at her and she looked at him, there had been an extra…something in the mix.

It was the summer she'd turned fourteen, and she'd never stood a chance. Because it was also the summer Lisa's father landed the bank manager's job in town and the Bartletts moved to Daylesford from Melbourne,

buying the big Victorian farmhouse at the end of the
street. Amy had taken one look at Lisa's flowing blond
hair and coltishly long, slender legs and known she was
special. So had Quinn, and before long the three of them
had been thick as thieves.

It had been the best kind of cultural exchange: they'd
shown her country-kid stuff like the best place to go
swimming at the lake and the shortcut to school through
Mrs. Brown's back paddock, and she'd taught them city-
kid skills like how to sneak into R-rated movies and ditch
school. It had been great. They'd called themselves the
three musketeers, thinking they were highly original.
Then...

Amy sat back in her seat and sighed. She figured it
said a lot about her messed-up psyche that she could still
remember with absolute clarity the day Lisa told her that
Quinn had kissed her. It had been nearly fifteen years but
the moment still loomed large on her mental horizon,
etched in acid in her memory.

IT WAS THE MIDDLE OF SUMMER and they were down at the
lake, sucking on flavored ice blocks in the stifling heat.
Amy was wearing last year's one-piece and feeling perfectly content until Lisa tugged off her T-shirt and skirt,
revealing a new red bikini. Lisa's budding breasts
stretched the Lycra triangles of her bra top, and her little
red pants seemed to make her legs go on forever. Amy
stared openly at her friend before looking down at her
own baby breasts, tamely covered by lots of aqua Lycra.
Then she shot a sideways glance at Quinn to see how he
was reacting.

They often did that—checked to see what the other
was thinking. But Quinn wasn't looking at Lisa. Not

directly, anyway. He was pretending to twist two strands of grass together while shooting quick, darting glances at Lisa from beneath the floppy fringe of his hair.

"Quinn, can you hold this for me?" Lisa asked, holding out her elasticated hair tie.

Amy wasn't quite sure why Lisa couldn't hold it herself—slide it onto her wrist or whatever—but Quinn took the tie and he and Amy watched as Lisa stood on the grassy slope, the sun behind her as she twisted her hair into a knot on the back of her head. She'd looked like she should be on TV, on one of those Coke ads where everyone was beautiful and laughing and having lots of fun.

When Lisa was satisfied she'd fixed her hair just right, she held out her hand and Quinn passed the hair tie over.

The expression in his eyes when he looked at Lisa this time made Amy uncomfortable. He looked...hungry. As though he wanted something from Lisa but was afraid to ask for it.

He shot to his feet. "I'm going swimming."

No sooner had he spoken than he was running down the slope. He barely slowed when he hit the water and started swimming toward the center of the lake.

Amy started to get to her feet, ready to join him, but Lisa grabbed her arm.

"Stay for a minute. There's something I want to tell you."

She sounded excited. She gave Amy's arm a little squeeze and Amy sank onto her towel.

"What's up?"

"Well. You know how I was helping Quinn with his French homework last night?"

"Yeah."

Lisa ran her hand down her smooth calf. She'd started

shaving this summer, as well as painting her toenails with her mom's polish.

"We were practicing verbs, same old, same old. Then all of a sudden he just grabbed me and kissed me." Lisa's blue eyes widened as she looked at Amy, inviting her to share her shock at what had happened.

Amy stilled. "Quinn kissed you?"

Lisa nodded, biting her lip.

"What was it like?" Amy had to force the words past the lump in her throat.

"Amazing. His lips are really strong. But soft. And when he put his tongue in my mouth, I nearly died."

Amy pulled her knees close to her chest and wrapped her arms around them. "Do you think—do you think you'll do it again?"

"If he wants to."

"Do you think he wants to?"

Lisa's gaze shifted to where Quinn was approaching the shore, his strong brown arms flashing in and out of the water. She frowned.

"I don't know. I hope so. I really like him. And not just like-like, you know? More than that."

Amy nodded. She knew exactly what Lisa meant. She was fourteen years old. She had more than like-liked Quinn for a whole year now. She'd lain awake at night imagining him kissing her, imagining what it would be like to feel his breath on her face, his lips on hers, his tongue in her mouth, his arms around her. He was her best friend, and she knew it was wrong to feel those kinds of things for him, but she couldn't help it.

And he'd kissed Lisa.

For a moment Amy couldn't breathe. There was a pain in her chest, as though someone was holding her too tightly.

Quinn had kissed Lisa. And now she knew what that look had meant, that hungry look: Quinn liked Lisa. More than like-liked. He wanted to kiss her again.

"It's really hot. I might go for a swim," Amy said, pushing herself to her feet.

"I'm going to start on that new book for English," Lisa said. She rolled onto her belly and reached for her school bag.

Amy stood staring down at her friend's slim body for a moment. If she had a red bikini, maybe Quinn would look at her like that…

But in her heart of hearts she knew it would take more than a red bikini to get Quinn to look at her the way he'd looked at Lisa.

She trudged to the edge of the lake and kept walking until the water was up to her armpits. As usual the water was icy cold but she hardly noticed as she closed her eyes and bent her knees and sank until she was entirely submerged.

Then she opened her mouth and screamed the rudest, nastiest word she knew, bubbles frothing against her face as she released all the air in her lungs. She waited until her lungs ached before resurfacing. She stared out across the lake, her chest rising and falling rapidly, wet hair clinging to her face. The sun glinted off the water, nearly blinding her.

She didn't care. She was too jealous and sad to care.

"Race you to the dock," Quinn said from behind her.

She whirled around and he splashed her full in the face. She spluttered and wiped her eyes. Quinn hooted with laughter.

Warmth filled her as she looked into his laughing face. Quinn might have kissed Lisa, but he was her best friend. That was something, right?

She retaliated with a mighty splash aimed straight up his nose and while he was spluttering for air took him up on his challenge by lunging forward and breaking into her fastest freestyle, her goal the distant dock. He was faster than her, but with a head start she could still make him sweat.

Her heart pumped and her breath came in gasps as she swam for her life.

It might not be so bad, she told herself. *Whatever is going on, it probably won't last long between them. None of the kids at school go out with each other for very long. It's not like they're going to get married or anything. I just have to wait it out.*

She caught a glimpse of the dark, wet wood of the dock ahead and glanced to her side to check on Quinn. He was nowhere to be seen and she risked a look over her shoulder, even though it would cost her speed. Surely she hadn't had that much of a head start on him?

But he wasn't there, either.

She stopped, her feet sinking into the soft mud of the lake bed. Some instinct made her push the wet hair from her eyes and squint over her shoulder to where their towels were spread on the grass.

Quinn stood in the shallows, accepting something from Lisa. A tube of suntan lotion. Lisa turned her back and gestured across her shoulders. Amy could imagine what she was saying. "I can't reach, would you mind?"

Quinn waded the rest of the way out of the lake. He must have felt Amy staring, because he glanced across to where she stood watching them.

He raised an arm, waved. "Be with you in a second, Ames."

Then he turned back to Lisa.

AMY TUGGED THE KEY from the ignition. Her fourteen-year-old self had been right about some things, wrong about others. Quinn and Lisa hadn't lasted that first time, but they'd gotten together twice more in their teen years and the last time had been for keeps. They'd applied to Sydney University together and left town together in Quinn's old brown Ford. Then they'd graduated, and the year Quinn landed a job in one of Sydney's top law firms, he'd asked Lisa to marry him. And she had accepted.

For all those years, Amy had sat on the sidelines, watching, waiting, aching. She'd made an art form out of hiding her yearning and jealousy. She'd gone out with other boys. She'd given her virginity to one of them, just to be done with the damned thing. No one had ever had a clue that she was in love with her best friend.

It had been better after Quinn and Lisa left for Sydney, easier—although harder, too, in some ways, losing two friends at once. But the relief had far outweighed the grief in the long term.

She'd hoped Quinn's departure would mean she'd stop loving him, but it hadn't. He was still very present in her life. He e-mailed regularly and called at least once a month, and if it wasn't him it was Lisa, filling her in on all the details of their life together. Study, exams, parties. Then work, the house they'd bought, the dinner parties they'd held. Amy had visited them once a year in Sydney and they'd all made a big deal out of how it was "just like old times."

But a person couldn't live forever on the edge of hope and longing, her face pressed to the glass, peering in and envying someone else's life, always wanting, never having. Amy had tried and failed, miserably.

Which was why she'd decided to cut herself free from

the past. Cut herself free from Quinn and Lisa. She'd lain awake in their guest bedroom when she'd visited two years ago and listened to the faint but unmistakable sound of Quinn and Lisa making love in their bedroom down the hall. She'd been sick with jealousy—literally. She'd stumbled to the bathroom and thrown up the rich three-course meal Lisa had cooked her. She made a decision in her heart that night. This was not the way she wanted to live her life.

She'd waited a few months before putting her decision into practice. First she eased off on phone calls. Then e-mails. Then she stopped communication altogether. Slowly, after she failed to reply to any and all correspondence, the attempts at contact had tapered off. At the time she'd been a little surprised at how easy it had been to slip away from their friendship. Now, of course, she knew they'd been dealing with their own crisis.

And now Quinn was home, and he was getting a divorce, and he wanted to pick their old friendship up where they'd left off.

Which left her…where, exactly?

A tap sounded on her car window and she started in her seat.

"Dad!" she said, pressing a hand to her pounding heart.

Her father peered in at her. "What are you doing, sitting out here in the cold on your own?"

A good question. A bloody good question.

"Nothing, Dad. Absolutely nothing," she said. Then she got out of her car and followed him inside.

QUINN WAS RESTLESS when he returned to the serviced apartment he'd rented for the weekend. He had a shower, turned on the television, stared at a pointless reality show, turned it off again. His body was tired, but his mind kept circling, thinking about the conversation he'd had with Amy, the theatre, his work, the myriad things that needed to be done now that he was going to stay in town for a while.

His decision to help Amy out at the council meeting had been so last-minute he hadn't had time to talk to his parents about using the family home. They were some-where in central Australia at the moment and not always in phone contact. It had been a while since he'd kept a spare key on his key ring, and even though he figured the Parkers probably had a copy, there had seemed little point in opening the house up for only two nights. Booking an apartment for the weekend had seemed the easiest option.

Plus there was something vaguely pathetic about a grown man on the brink of divorce returning home to sleep in his childhood bedroom.

But now that he was staying longer, it made sense to use the house. He dialed his mother's cell and was put straight through to voice mail. He left a message telling her his plans, then he dragged out his laptop and plugged into the apartment complex's broadband.

As soon as he logged in he saw there was an e-mail from Duffy Calhoun, one of the firm's family law spe-cialists. Quinn had approached him to handle the divorce a few months ago, and as far as he knew things were well in hand. Legally, couples needed to have been separated for a year before a divorce could be issued in Australia. There were ways around this—cheating the separation date, for example—but neither he nor Lisa had been in a rush. In another four weeks, the full twelve months would be up and they could file the papers. It was almost over.

He saw from the time stamp that Duffy's e-mail had

arrived after he'd flown down to Melbourne. He clicked on the icon and frowned as he read his colleague's message. Apparently Duffy had called Lisa's lawyer twice during the week and had yet to hear back. Duffy wasn't sending up a flare yet, but he wanted to warn Quinn that in the world of divorce negotiations it usually wasn't a good sign when the opposing counsel stopped returning phone calls.

Quinn leaned back in bed. As far as he was concerned, the divorce couldn't be more clear-cut—a fifty-fifty split, straight down the middle. They'd both contributed equally to the mortgage, and there were no children or pets. What more could Lisa possibly want? Surely she wasn't going to come after his retirement fund?

He rejected the thought as soon as it occurred. While he and Lisa weren't inviting each other over for dinner, things weren't acrimonious, either. Even though he knew she valued anything that conferred status—fancy houses, fancier cars—he didn't think she had it in her to be so viciously acquisitive.

He sent a quick reply to Duffy asking him to keep trying Lisa's lawyer. They couldn't file for a decree of dissolution of marriage until she'd signed her share of the papers, but Quinn was convinced the lawyer not calling back was only an oversight.

He switched the light off around midnight. By two he was still staring at the ceiling. Sleep had become a rare commodity in his life in the past year. He was getting used to being awake when most of the world wasn't, but he didn't like it. Nothing like an early hours vigil to make the empty side of the bed seem colder and emptier.

He rolled onto his side. Back in the old days if he'd had trouble sleeping, he would have opened his bedroom window and thrown pebbles—he'd kept a supply in his room for that purpose—at Amy's window across the way until she was awake, too. She'd have come to her window, bleary-eyed and cranky, then they would have used the walkie-talkies they'd bought with their allowances to plan tomorrow's mad scheme until one or the other of them drifted off to sleep.

He smiled. Man, he and Amy had done some crazy shit over the years. There was the time they'd made a go-cart out of scrap wood and the wheels from Amy's in-line skates. They'd taken it to the steepest street in town, strapped themselves in and pushed off. He'd wound up with a black eye and a chipped tooth and Amy had grazed her knees and broken a finger.

Despite the pain at the end of that hair-raising rocket down the hillside, the thing that stood out the most in his mind was the way Amy had clutched his arms and whooped with joy as the wind whipped at their faces. She'd been absolutely fearless.

In hindsight, it was a wonder they'd both survived childhood, the way they'd egged each other on.

The smile faded from his mouth as he thought about the conversation they'd had tonight. He hoped they'd cleared the air. She was important to him. Very. And he was determined to fix whatever had gone wrong between them.

THE REAR DOOR to the Grand was open when Amy pulled into the parking lot the next morning. It was only seven-thirty, but she figured Quinn must have beaten her there.

She thought about the day ahead, working alongside him. Laughing with him. Sharing with him. She knew it probably made her a particularly sick and twisted kind of masochist, but a part of her was enormously pleased that he was here to share these first formative days. Even though she knew having him so close and working with him so intimately was probably going to drive her a little bit nuts. The Grand was her dream, and Quinn was the man she loved. There was something very bittersweet about the two great passions of her life sitting alongside each other, even if it was only for five measly weeks.

And when Quinn went back to Sydney…well, she'd pick herself up and dust herself off the way she always did. And who knew, maybe a miracle would occur while they worked together to restore the Grand to its former glory. Maybe after all these years her heart would be able to let Quinn go and he could become simply her dear, beloved friend. Nothing more.

She smiled a little grimly. *Good luck with that one.*

She got out of her car, took a deep breath and strode into the Grand, game face firmly on.

"Trying to make me look bad, Whitfield?" she said as she entered the theatre from the corridor.

She stopped in her tracks when she saw the man standing in the middle of the space, his head tilted back as he studied the ceiling. He was wearing a dark double-breasted suit, even though it was a Sunday, and his shiny red tie matched his florid cheeks.

"Mr. Ulrich," she said.

What the hell was he doing here?

"Hope you don't mind. I saw the back door was open and I thought I'd step inside to wait for you since it looked like it might rain."

Amy narrowed her eyes. It was clear and sunny outside and Barry needed a slit cut into the back of his suit jacket to accommodate his dorsal fin.

"Actually, I do mind. And the back door wasn't open."

Ulrich's face creased into a complacent, confident half smile. "Unsecured, then. Not the smartest move, putting all these priceless heritage-listed architectural features at risk."

Amy wished she was wearing something a little more intimidating than her purple-and-green-striped long-sleeved T-shirt, jeans and sparkly hot pink sneakers. She really wished she hadn't put her hair in pigtails this morning.

"I really don't think it's appropriate that you're here. I'd like you to leave."

Ulrich's lips twitched as though he found her endlessly amusing.

"I want to talk to you," he said.

"Then we can make an appointment to talk another time. I'm busy now."

"You don't look very busy to me."

"Well, I am. So if you don't mind…"

She gestured toward the door. Ulrich didn't budge. She didn't like the way he looked at her, as though she was a fly he wanted to swat. Fear goosed its way down her spine. She knew he'd never dare touch her, but she couldn't help feeling vulnerable, standing here alone in the semidark with a man who clearly wished her to hell.

"So predictable, Ames. Bet you were here at sparrow's fart, right?"

She spun toward the door as Quinn entered, two coffee cups and a white bakery bag in hand. Never had she been so glad to see him.

There was a slight hitch in his step when he saw Ulrich, then he continued to her side.

"I was just explaining to Mr. Ulrich that the Grand is mine now and that I don't want him entering the property when I'm not around."

She opened her eyes meaningfully as she looked at

Quinn. He frowned and she knew he'd gotten the message that Ulrich had been here before she'd arrived.

Quinn handed Amy one of the coffees, his warm fingers brushing her cold ones as they swapped grips on the cup. Instantly the shaky feeling inside her faded. It was impossible to feel intimidated when Quinn was by her side.

Quinn took a sip of his coffee before he spoke.

"As I'm sure you're aware, Barry, trespassing is a criminal offence," he said. His tone was friendly, relaxed, but there was a hard light in his eyes.

Ulrich laughed. "Relax, mate. I'm not here to do any harm. In fact, I'm here to make Ms. Parker the offer of a lifetime."

"I'm not interested in listening to any offers," Amy said.

"You haven't even heard what it is yet," Ulrich said. "How do you know you're not interested?"

"Because I'm not interested," Amy repeated.

Ulrich carried on as though she hadn't spoken, pulling some papers from his suit pocket. "I want to buy the Grand off you. I've got a contract here—"

"No." She crossed her arms over her chest.

"I'm willing to give you a hundred thousand more than you paid for it."

"Amy's given you her answer," Quinn said. "Nobody likes a poor loser, Ulrich."

The developer's pale blue eyes narrowed. "Don't be a silly girl. Look at the deal. Talk it over with your boyfriend. Think about how many nice pairs of shoes you can buy yourself with a hundred thousand dollars of easy profit."

"Enough. It's time for you to go," Quinn said.

Ulrich didn't take his eyes off Amy. "Take the contract."

He thrust the contract at her like a weapon, his color high. She glared at him, arms still locked over her chest.

"No."

"Take it."

Suddenly she was staring at Quinn's broad shoulders as he stepped between them.

"You can walk out or I can throw you out. Want to flip a coin over it?" He sounded like a stranger, his voice was so cold and angry.

Ulrich hesitated a moment, then he said something under his breath and walked away, heels striking the wooden floor sharply with each step.

"That man—" She broke off. She was so angry she didn't know where to put herself.

The way Ulrich had looked at her…

His smug arrogance…

Quinn lifted the white bakery bag. "I bought almond croissants. With any luck they're still warm."

"Croissants? Are you kidding?" She wanted to spit nails, not consume baked goods.

He tucked his coffee into the crook of his arm and unfolded the top of the bag. He pulled out a sugar-dusted pastry and offered it to her. "Have a croissant."

She shook her head impatiently. The last thing she felt like was eating.

"Ames, don't give him the satisfaction of rattling you."

"I'm already rattled."

Quinn put some gravel in his voice, creating a reasonable proximity of Ulrich's impatient bark. "Take the croissant, Amy."

His eyes were laughing at her, inviting her to join in.

"Quinn…"

"Take it. Take it, I say."

He thrust it toward her melodramatically. Despite herself, she felt her mouth twitch at the corners. "Stop it."

"You know what you have to do to make that happen."

She rolled her eyes and plucked the croissant from his hand. "I'm still angry," she said as she pulled off a chunk of buttery pastry.

"Sure. But consider this—he's a douche bag, you own the Grand and we'll install a big-ass lock on the door today so he can never get in here again. Still want to waste half an hour fuming over the guy?"

She chewed and swallowed. "No."

"That's my girl," Quinn said, slinging an arm around her shoulder.

His body was hard along her side. Her stupid heart gave an excited kick in her chest.

"If you're trying to out-patronize Ulrich you're off to a good start," she said, trying to ignore the tumult that had started up within her body.

He looked at her, tucked under his arm. "Come on, I'm not even close. I haven't even mentioned pretty shoes yet. The guy's a pro."

He had a small milk mustache from the foam on his latte. Before she could stop herself, she reached up to wipe the foam away with her thumb. His stubble scraped across her skin, the roughness a startling contrast to the silky firmness of his upper lip.

Her belly tightened. How many times had she imagined those lips kissing her?

And not just on the mouth.

"There was a time when you'd have let me walk around all day wearing that," he said.

"Those were the days."

Feeling overwhelmed, she shrugged out from beneath his arm.

"Before I forget, Mom asked me to ask you over for dinner tonight," she said, concentrating on brushing powdered sugar off her T-shirt so she wouldn't have to look him in the eye. "She's cooking lasagna to celebrate me buying the Grand."

Quinn's face lit up. "I would crawl over broken glass for one of your mom's lasagnas." He rubbed his hands together in boyish anticipation.

"Fortunately all you have to do is turn up and be mildly entertaining."

"I'll brush up on my witty anecdotes after lunch."

"That should do it."

He tugged on one of her pigtails before turning away to dump his empty cup in the garbage. She stared at his broad shoulders, then her gaze dropped to the firm roundness of his ass.

Maybe one day she would learn to love him as a friend, and only as a friend. But that day was not going to be today.

Not by a long shot.

QUINN CLIMBED down the last rung on the extension ladder and dropped the bucket and sponge he'd been holding to the floor. He tilted his neck to the left, then the right, then circled his shoulders. He'd been scrubbing walls for four hours now. He and Amy had borrowed the extension ladders from her parents' store and picked up a load of primer and paint and wall wash, then they'd started on the long process of prepping the walls for painting.

Amy had taken the upper and lower foyers and the balcony section, while he was tackling the main theatre. He rolled his shoulders again. He was going to feel it in his arms tomorrow, without a doubt.

The tinny sound of The Bangles' "Walk Like an Egyptian" segued into The Eagles' "Hotel California." Finally, some man's music. He crossed to the beaten-up stereo to crank the volume. He'd spotted the old unit in Amy's father's office at the store. Amy had raised an eyebrow when he'd loaded it into her station wagon along with their other supplies.

"Hope Dad knows you've got that," she'd said. "He lives to listen to the horse races on his breaks."

"He handed it over with his blessing."

"Sure he did."

"He did. He understands the importance of listening to bad eighties rock while doing physical labor. Plus I offered him a case of beer."

"Now *that* I believe."

He'd been keeping an eye on her since this morning, but she seemed to have recovered from Ulrich's impromptu visit. He'd played it cool for her sake, but he'd been hard-pressed not to grab Ulrich by the throat when the developer had tried to force his unwanted offer on her. Quinn didn't think he'd ever forget the flash of relief he'd seen in her eyes when he'd walked through the door, coffees in hand. Even though he knew she'd rather eat a whole jar of olives than admit it, Ulrich scared her. As well he might. The guy was a bully, used to barking out orders and having them followed. He didn't like being crossed, and he definitely didn't like losing out to a woman wearing sparkly pink sneakers.

Quinn gripped the sides of the big extension ladder

and hefted it several feet to the right. First thing tomorrow, he was going to set things in motion to move up the settlement date. A contract of sale was one thing, but he wasn't going to rest easy until Amy was actually holding the deed to the Grand in her hands. The sooner he could make that happen, the better.

He grabbed the bucket and was about to climb the ladder when he heard Amy swear loudly over the top of the music.

He glanced toward the balcony, but she was hidden from his view.

"You okay?" he called.

He heard nothing but the sound of jangling guitar and the chorus of the song. He hesitated. Amy would probably be making a hell of a lot more noise if she'd hurt herself, but he decided to check on her anyway, since it was nearly time for lunch. She'd work straight through if she had her way, but he'd seen a gourmet burger place farther up the street when he'd walked to the Grand this morning and was keen to give it a try. Even if he had to drag her kicking and screaming all the way.

He exited to the foyer and started up the wide marble stairs.

"You've seriously got to learn some new swear words, Ames," he said as he mounted the last few steps to the upper foyer. The rest of his speech died in his throat when he saw her.

Her back was turned and she was peeling her sopping wet T-shirt over her head. She clearly hadn't heard him because she didn't so much as glance over her shoulder as she let the T-shirt slap to the ground. She was wearing a red-and-white polka-dot bra underneath and he stared at her slim back and told himself to walk away.

Then she turned in profile and he saw that her bra cups were trimmed with lace where they curved over her small, high breasts. He could just make out the shadow of her nipples behind the sheer fabric. Time seemed to slow and stretch. Then she bent and picked up her sweater, pulling it over her head, and the peep show was over.

Because that was exactly what it was: a peep show.

She had no idea he was watching. And he should have either retreated or announced himself the moment that he'd realized what was happening.

But he hadn't.

CHAPTER FIVE

ANY MOMENT NOW Amy was going to turn and see him.

Ten seconds too late, he took a step backward, then another, then a third and fourth until he was halfway down the stairs and below Amy's sight line.

He paused, one hand on the balustrade. He should go straight up and apologize to her. Right now. Explain what had happened. Make a joke out of it.

He could feel heat rising into his face. He imagined himself telling her that he'd been about to say something, to clear his throat and let her know he was there but then she'd turned and he'd seen her breasts, seen the shadow of her nipples through all that lace, and he'd been too busy wondering what color they were and if they were as small and perfect as the rest of her to do the decent thing….

He turned and descended the stairs to the foyer. The front doors were standing open and he stepped out onto the street and sucked in some fresh air.

Half a dozen memories nudged at the back of his mind, wanting in. This wasn't the first time he'd looked at his best friend and felt desire, after all.

He stared up Vincent Street, but he wasn't seeing the Sunday strollers and pottering tourists. Instead, he was lost in an old memory: Amy standing in her bedroom

window, her silhouette cast into sharp relief against her
drawn blind thanks to her bedside lamp. Her hands reaching behind her back to undo the clasp on her bra. The
straps sliding down her arms. The pointed tips of her
bare breasts. The guilt and confusion and desire he'd felt,
watching her from his bedroom next door.

He'd been fourteen, completely unprepared for the
demands and urges of his newly rampant teenage body.
He could still remember the baffled outrage he'd felt at
the time, as though the world had pulled a fast one on him.
One minute Amy had been his best buddy, the next she'd
had breasts and he'd started noticing weird things about
her. The way she always smelled good, like sunshine and
green apples. The way her eyelashes cast shadows on her
cheeks when she was lying in the sun. The round firmness
of her ass whenever she was walking in front of him.

He'd started having dreams about her around that time,
too. About the two of them lying in the grass together at
the bottom of her parents' yard. Sometimes they'd be lying
there talking and laughing like always. Other times he'd
look across at her and she'd be looking back at him and
he'd roll toward her and kiss her. A few times she kissed
him back and he couldn't believe how good it felt. Her
mouth so warm and wet. But most of the time she pushed
him away and the look in her eyes when she stared at him
sent him groping for consciousness, his heart pounding.

How many nights had he lain panting in the dark in
his bedroom, his body thrumming with illicit desire for
his best friend as he told himself over and over that the
disgust on her face was not real, that he hadn't really
kissed her, that it was all just a dream?

A really dumb, stupid, wrong dream.

He'd had dreams about Lisa around that time, too. But

the truth was, for a long time it had been Amy he'd lusted after, not Lisa. Amy, the girl next door. His best friend.

Quinn glanced toward the Grand.

For the first time in his adult life he wondered if she'd ever looked at him and seen him as a man instead of a friend. Whether she'd ever let herself go there…

What are you doing, man?

He'd done a lot of dumb things since his marriage had broken up. No way was he adding ruining his friendship with Amy to the list simply because he was feeling nostalgic and horny and confused.

She was his friend. End of story. She'd be appalled if she knew he was out here talking himself out of the world's most inappropriate hard-on because he'd seen her in her bra. Or she'd laugh herself sick at the idea of the two of them together.

Either way, it wasn't worth the risk of destroying their friendship. Making things weird. So what if he found her sexually attractive? It meant dick when he put it into the balance against all that she meant to him, all the memories they shared, all the trust that connected them.

Only an idiot would indulge his desires when the price was so high.

Moment of madness over, he headed back inside.

"Fantastic lasagna, Mrs. P.," Quinn said.

Amy gave him a look. "Stop being such a suck-up. And pass the parmesan."

"Quinn can compliment me on my cooking any time he likes, Amy," her mother said.

They were seated around the family table in Amy's parents' kitchen, the smell of tomatoes and onions rich in the air.

"You know he's just angling for a bigger serving of apple crumble," Amy said.

Quinn widened his eyes innocently. "Is there apple crumble for dessert?"

"You know there is. You saw Mom put it into the oven," she said.

Quinn handed her the cheese, a smile playing around his mouth. "I didn't notice."

Her mother patted him on the arm. "Don't worry, Quinn, I know how much you like my apple crumble. I made plenty, just to be safe."

Her father wiped his mouth with his napkin. "So, Quinn. How are things going with work? Your father told me you made partner last year. That's a pretty big deal, isn't it?"

"It was nice to have it settled," Quinn said.

Amy nudged him under the table. "Listen to Mr. Modesty. He's the youngest partner ever at his law firm. And they've been in business for over a hundred and fifty years."

Quinn frowned at her. "How do you know that?"

"Your mother. Who else?"

Quinn shook his head ruefully. "I should have known."

Her mother clucked her tongue and waved her fork at him. "Don't deny your mother the right to brag, Quinn. It's one of the few perks of childbirth."

Amy took a sip of her wine, watching Quinn over the rim of her glass. It was strange seeing him in her parents' kitchen again after all these years. The setting hadn't changed—her mother's prized blue-and-white decor had remained the same for decades—but he had. There was a new reserve to him. He was more cautious, a little slower to laugh than he used to be.

"Louise tells me you also bought a new house?" her mother asked. "She said they stayed with you last year and that it looks like something out of *House and Garden* magazine."

Amy listened as Quinn described his new house to her parents. He and Lisa had moved not long after her last visit so she hadn't seen the new place. It sounded big and expensive. Very Lisa.

When they'd exhausted the topic of the house they moved on to her parents' business, then Amy's plans for the Grand.

Her mother ushered them into the living room after that while she served up dessert and coffee. Her father went off to dig up a bottle of scotch and Amy set a match to the wood stacked in the fireplace.

She could feel Quinn watching her as she fed more kindling to the flames.

"Thanks," he said after a short silence.

"For giving you a hard time over the apple crumble?"

"For warning your folks about the divorce."

"Oh. That." She glanced at him out of the corners of her eyes. "Mad at me for blabbing?"

"No. I think it's cute you were trying to protect me."

She screwed up her face in disgust. "I wasn't trying to protect you. I was saving you from killing the conversation with your sad sack story."

Quinn smiled enigmatically. "So transparent, Parker."

She pointed the fire poker at him. "And don't call me cute, okay? You know I hate that."

Her father returned with a bottle of scotch as her mom ferried in bowls of crumble. Amy rolled her eyes when she saw how big Quinn's portion was.

"If there's any justice in the world, you'll be as sick as a dog after that."

Quinn leaned across and kissed her mother's cheek.

"You're a goddess, Mrs. P."

"Brown nose," Amy muttered under her breath.

Quinn smiled beatifically as he dug into his dessert.

Afterward, Amy cleared the plates and helped her mother stack the dishwasher.

"Such a shame," her mother said out of nowhere as Amy was shaking detergent into the washer.

Amy shot her mother a quizzical look.

"The divorce," her mother said in a stage whisper, her eyes sliding to the living room door.

"He knows you know, Mom. It's not a state secret. You can talk about it if you like."

"It's none of my business," her mother said quickly. "I just think it's a shame. He's a lovely, lovely man. I'm sure he was a wonderful husband."

Amy stared out the kitchen window into the dark garden, thinking about what she'd seen of Lisa and Quinn's life together.

"He was."

"Well, I'm sure he'll do better second time around."

The dishwasher door slipped out of Amy's hands and slammed shut with a rattle of glassware.

"Second time? He's barely divorced and you've already married him off again."

"Only being realistic, sweetheart. Some smart woman will snap him up. And it won't take long, either."

Amy stared at her mother, wanting to object but knowing her mom was right. Quinn was a great guy. The best. Gorgeous, smart, funny.

Single.

There'd be a queue forming the moment he started dating again.

Bloody hell.

As if watching Quinn get married once had not been hard enough. She was going to have to do it all over again. Watch him fall in love. Listen to him talk about his future wife. The bachelor party, the wedding… All of it, all over again.

She closed her eyes for a long beat.

"Amy. You've gone so pale. Are you all right?"

"I'm fine." Amy opened her eyes. "I think I'm a bit tired. It was a big day."

"You have to pace yourself. I know you've been panting to get into that old theatre and fix it up, but you need to look after yourself."

"I just need a good night's sleep."

And a reset button on her heart.

When they returned to the living room her father was asking Quinn for advice on a contract with one of his major suppliers. Amy listened to them talk for another fifteen minutes before making her excuses. It was too hard sitting across from Quinn, thinking about what her mother had said.

She drove three streets over to her own cottage and shivered as she entered the front hall. As usual, her place was freezing, thanks to the fact that there was no central heating. The price she paid for keeping her rent down.

She turned on the small fan heater in her bedroom and stripped for the shower. She was going to wash off the sweat and grime of the day, put on her warmest flannel pajamas and go to bed thinking about the Grand and how great it was going to look when she'd completed the restoration. She was not going to brood or sulk over Quinn. She'd wasted too many years already. Quinn not loving her was not a tragedy. It wasn't. It was disappointing. Sad. But it was not the defining fact of her life. She refused to let it be.

She was naked and ready to walk into her ensuite bathroom when her phone rang. She glanced toward the shower longingly before scooping up her phone.

"Amy speaking."

There was a long silence. Then she heard someone swallow.

"Ames. It's me."

Amy sank onto the edge of her bed. "Lisa."

"Surprise!" Lisa said with ironic brightness. "I bet you weren't expecting to hear from me. Especially after what Quinn's probably told you."

Amy scrambled to assemble her thoughts. How did Lisa know Quinn was in town? Had he told her? Were they still in contact?

"He hasn't told me that much, to be honest. Just that you two are getting a divorce," Amy said.

She could hear the coolness in her own voice. She couldn't help it, but she felt guilty for it, all the same. Lisa was her friend, too, no matter what had happened between her and Quinn.

"I'm sure he told you more than that." Lisa's voice was so faint Amy had to press the handset to her ear to hear.

"He told me that you were with someone else."

"That I had an affair, you mean."

"Yes."

"Do you hate me?"

Amy was shivering. She leaned across the bed to drag her quilt over her shoulders. "No. Of course I don't."

But it was impossible to pretend that she didn't feel differently toward her old friend.

"But you disapprove, right? You think I'm a dirty bitch for messing up Quinn's life?" Her speech was slurred.

"Are you okay?" Amy asked, concerned. Lisa sounded deeply unhappy.

"Sure. I'm great. New man, new house, new life. What's not to love?" There was a short pause, then Lisa sighed heavily. When she spoke again her tone was more sincere, less brittle. "Sorry, Ames. I'm just… How are you? We haven't spoken for ages."

Because she wasn't sure what else to do, Amy gave her old friend a quick rundown on what had been happening in her life: the Grand, Quinn's part in helping her win the fight with the council, the renovations she had planned. It was awkward and uncomfortable, stilted in a way things had never been with Lisa before.

There was a short pause when she'd finished.

"And how is Quinn? Last time I saw him he'd lost a bit of weight," Lisa said.

"Well, he's doesn't complain when I boss him around, which is a good thing, right?" Amy joked.

"Ames, has he mentioned anyone? Another woman?"

Here we go. Was this why Lisa had called? To fish for information on Quinn?

"Lis, I really don't want to play piggy in the middle, you know?"

"Please. I just need to know this one thing." She sounded desperate. "Is he seeing anyone?"

Amy tugged the quilt tighter. "I'm sorry, Lis."

"All right. I understand. You and Quinn were always close. I get why you'd pick him over me. I'm the dirty wrongdoer, right?"

"It's got nothing to do with choosing sides. If you want to know how Quinn is, who he's dating, whatever, you need to talk to him, not me. I'm not a marriage counselor or a go-between."

"It's okay, Amy. I'd probably be the same myself. Good for you for standing by him. If it's not pushing our friendship too much, I'd appreciate it if you didn't mention this call to Quinn."

"Lisa—"

But it was too late, she was listening to the dial tone. *Shit.*

Amy threw the phone to one side and made a frustrated sound in her throat. What had Lisa expected from her? A full report on Quinn's comings and goings? An intimate recounting of all his conversations?

It wasn't fair of Lisa to try to trade off their friendship to pump Amy for information. In fact, it was uncool in the extreme and Amy was tempted to call Lisa back and tell her as much.

Two things stopped her: the fact that she'd been lying through her teeth when she'd said she wasn't on anyone's side, and the memory of that small, ugly moment not long after Quinn had told her he was getting a divorce when she'd consciously registered the fact that he was free to love again and a part of her had rejoiced.

She wasn't exactly a shining example of virtue in this situation, after all.

She was covered in gooseflesh by now and she took the quilt with her as she crossed to the ensuite. She waited until the water was steaming hot before tossing the quilt into her bedroom and stepping beneath the shower.

The water was hot and hard. She turned her face into the spray and held her breath. Only then did she allow herself to ask the question that had been echoing inside her since Lisa's call.

If Lisa wanted to try again, would Quinn take her back?

Her gut said no, that Quinn was too hurt, too angry to forgive two years of lies and betrayal. But what did she know, really, at the end of the day? Quinn and Lisa had been together for a long time. Who knew how far and how deep their connection went? Marriages had recovered from worse blows, she was sure.

It doesn't matter. It's none of your business. If they get back together or not is irrelevant. It doesn't change anything for you. Not a thing.

God, how she needed to hang on to that reality.

She also needed to decide whether it would be a bigger betrayal of Quinn to tell him Lisa had called or to do as Lisa asked and keep it a secret.

So much for not brooding.

THEY WERE SITTING on the edge of the dock down at the lake. It took Quinn a moment to recognize it as the night before his wedding. Amy sat opposite him in a pair of cut-off jeans and a tank top, her hair pulled back in a ponytail. They were drinking Coronas with slices of lime in the neck of the bottle. The air was warm, the moon full.

"Tomorrow's going to be a great day. The best day of my life," he said.

Amy smiled and nodded. "You're going to be a great husband."

"I know."

They both laughed because he sounded like such a cocky son of a bitch.

"You finally going to come up to Sydney and visit us once we're back from the honeymoon?" He and Lisa had been bugging Amy for ages to visit them in Sydney. She always had an excuse.

"You guys aren't going to want me hanging around.

I've heard all those newlywed stories." She shuddered theatrically.

He tilted his bottle toward her. "You need to get out of town. See the big wide world."

"Don't make me sound like some kind of hick. Melbourne is an hour away, in case you'd forgotten."

"We miss you, Ames."

She stared at him. Then she braced her arms on the dock and pushed herself to her feet.

"It's too hot. Let's swim."

He almost choked on his beer as she reached for the waistband of her tank top and pulled it over her head. She was wearing a red-and-white polka-dot bra underneath. He could see her nipples. He told himself to stop looking, but she was smoothing her hands down her belly to the stud on her cutoffs.

"What's wrong, Quinn? Not hot enough for you?"

Her voice was low, husky. She didn't sound like Amy. Not the Amy he knew.

She was watching him, her eyes heavy-lidded and smoky. She popped the stud. Her zip hissed as she slid it down. Then she tucked her thumbs into the waistband and pushed her cutoffs over her hips. She was wearing matching panties and he could see a shadow of blond hair through the lace.

"You're getting married tomorrow. Haven't you ever wondered what it would be like between us?"

She stepped closer, standing between his bent knees. He looked up, his gaze traveling over her thighs, her belly, her breasts. He was so hard it hurt, his erection straining against the fabric of his cargo shorts.

He set his beer on the dock. Then he lifted his hand toward her.

Just one touch. To see if she was as soft and warm and lovely as he'd always—

QUINN JERKED AWAKE. The sheets were damp with sweat and he was as hard as a rock, his heart pounding.

He blinked, fragments from his dream lingering in his mind's eye.

What the hell was that all about?

But he knew. The dream had been a tangled mess of memory and fantasy. Those stolen moments from the upper foyer today grafted onto the night six years ago when he and Amy had gotten drunk before his wedding. Needless to say, Amy had not stripped for him that night. They'd gone swimming, sure, but she'd jumped into the lake in her cutoffs and tank top. And he'd certainly never tried to touch her.

He kicked off the sheet, trying to cool his body.

He was thirty, not fourteen. Long past the age when horny dreams and fantasies were commonplace. Especially about his best friend.

Gradually his heart slowed. He didn't understand what was going on, why he was suddenly thinking about Amy in this way. It wasn't as though he hadn't slept with anyone else since he and Lisa broke up. Hell, for a while there he'd been in serious running for man-whore of the year. There was no good reason for him to be having these thoughts about Amy.

He rolled out of bed and reached for his clothes. Five minutes later he was outside, hands deep in his coat pockets, shoulders hunched as he walked up the street.

Fog had come with the night and the streetlights stood out like small, glowing lighthouses in the gloom. He walked toward the hardware store, then did a lap of the lake. He felt like the last man on earth, utterly alone.

The lights were on in the bakery when he walked up to Vincent Street, steam condensing on the windows. He wondered what time it was. Three? Four? He was turning to head back to his apartment when something flashed in his peripheral vision. He stopped and stared across the road at the Grand. The front windows were dark. As they should be.

Still, he'd seen something.

He crossed the street and peered through the glass doors. Adrenaline kicked through his belly as he saw a thin flashlight beam crawl across the wall of the theatre, just visible through the archway.

Someone was in there.

He pulled his phone from his back pocket. He was about to dial emergency when it occurred to him that maybe it was Amy inside. Maybe, like him, she'd been unable to sleep.

He broke into a jog and turned into the alley that ran along the side of the theatre. When he reached the corner, he slowed and flattened his back to the wall. If it really was Amy inside, he was going to feel like an enormous dick playing *Starsky and Hutch* out here in the middle of the night.

He eased around the corner and saw immediately that the rear door had been kicked in. The padlock he'd installed when they'd gotten back from their supply trip had ripped a substantial chunk out of the door frame before it had given way. Whoever was inside, they'd wanted in, big-time.

He ducked back into the alley and called emergency.

"Please state the name of the emergency service you require," the operator said into his ear.

"Police."

"I'm putting you through now, sir. Please hold the line."

There was a click, then a short pause. Quinn used the moment to pull his thoughts together. A man came on the line.

"Victorian Police. What's your emergency?"

"My name is Quinn Whitfield. I'm outside the Grand Picture Theatre in Daylesford. Someone has broken into the premises. They're still inside. I need you to get the local police here, stat."

"Please hold the line while I alert the local police, sir."

Quinn waited for long moments, his mind ticking over. There was no way the cops would get here for another ten minutes. Someone intent on destruction could do a lot of damage in that time.

He eased around the corner again and ducked his head through the open doorway. It was pitch-black, which meant the door at the other end must be closed. He hesitated a moment, then made a decision. This was Amy's dream. No way was he going to stand by while it was trashed.

He ended the call and slid his phone into his pocket, then he started up the corridor, moving as soundlessly as possible.

He could feel his heart pounding like a tom-tom in his chest. It had been years since he'd been in a fight, but he figured he still knew how to hurt someone if he had to.

His outstretched hand hit the surface of the door. He found the handle. Took a deep breath. Jerked the door open.

"Oi! What the hell do you think you're doing?" he bellowed at the top of his lungs.

Two flashlight beams swung toward him, blinding

him, then suddenly it was dark. Quinn blinked furiously, trying to force his eyes to adjust. He heard the scuff of footsteps and braced himself. He was standing in front of the only viable exit; they wanted to get out, they had to come through him.

He squared up. All he had to do was keep these guys occupied until the cops showed up. Five, six minutes, max.

A dark shape came at him. He dropped his shoulder and lunged forward, aiming for the solar plexus. Something hard hit him in the chest—the flashlight, maybe—then he was on the ground grappling with someone who felt a hell of a lot bigger and heavier than him. His fist connected with a jaw. He took a blow to the gut, another to the neck. He gasped for air, caught a handful of greasy hair with one hand and a fistful of clothing with the other and attempted to force his assailant onto his back.

Pain exploded in his side and he shied away from it. A kick. How…? Another blow landed on his ribs. Then he understood the second guy had joined the fray. He released his grip on the first guy, shoved him backward. Tried to scramble to his feet—and stepped straight into a swinging fist. He flew backward, his head slamming into the wall. Disoriented and winded, he struggled to keep his feet.

A siren split through the night, then a flash of blue whipped past as a cop car sped by the front of the cinema.

"Cops! Go! Go!" someone yelled.

Footsteps pounded down the corridor toward the rear exit. Quinn started after them. Dizziness hit him when he was halfway up the corridor. He wavered on his feet. Must have knocked his head harder than he'd thought. He found the wall with an outstretched hand. The world still swung crazily. He put his back to the wall and slid down until his butt hit the floor.

Better. The world was much steadier down here.

If he could catch his breath... He closed his eyes.

His jaw felt like it had been hit with a sledgehammer. Something trickled down his face. He took a swipe at it with his fingers.

Footsteps scuffed in the corridor. He opened his eyes just as a brilliant flashlight beam found him. He flinched away from the brightness.

"Police! Stay where you are and put your hands on your head."

"My name's Quinn Whitfield," he said. "I'm the guy who called it in." Still, he put his hands on his head.

It took five minutes for him to tell his story. The cop waited until he had confirmation from his radio before relaxing his vigilant stance.

"You need me to call an ambulance? Looks like you're bleeding," the cop said, playing the beam over Quinn's face.

"I'm fine."

"Should have waited for us to get here. Stupid coming in here alone."

Quinn fingered his sore jaw. *Tell me something I don't know, buddy.*

The cop's radio crackled to life. Quinn strained to understand what was said but it was too garbled.

"Did you catch them?" Quinn asked.

The cop shook his head, looking as disappointed as Quinn felt. "We're still in pursuit."

The cop aimed the beam up the corridor toward the cinema.

"There much damage inside?"

Quinn braced his arm against the wall and pushed himself to his feet.

"Don't know."

The cop strode forward, his powerful flashlight beam cutting through the darkness. Quinn was close enough to hear him swear softly under his breath when he entered the cinema.

Quinn stopped in the doorway, speechless. More than half the cans of primer and top coat they'd bought had been pried open and pushed over. White paint spread across the floor in an ever-widening pool, thick and relentless. Two of the wall sconces had been ripped from the wall and were hanging by their wiring, their glass shades shattered on the floors. Ugly graffiti sprawled across the walls in vivid red paint.

Amy was going to freak when she saw this.

He dug in his pocket for his cell phone. Miraculously, it was still in one piece, albeit with a crack across the screen.

If there was some way to fix this, make it all disappear before Amy had to see it, he would. But he couldn't, and she needed to be told.

"Quinn? What time is it?" a sleepy voice asked.

He could picture her, hair tousled, face soft from sleep. He rubbed the bridge of his nose, hating being the bearer of bad tidings.

"Ames, there's been a break-in at the Grand. I'm here with the cops, and there's a ton of wet paint on the floor that we're going to need to clean up somehow."

There was a short silence. "I'll be there in five."

CHAPTER SIX

AMY MADE IT IN TEN, dressed in jeans and sneakers and a pajama top, her flashlight in hand. She walked through the door and stopped in her tracks when she saw the spreading pool of paint.

Quinn had been leaning against the wall while he waited but he straightened when he saw her.

"My God," she said after a long beat. "What a pack of assholes."

Any other woman would have been hysterical, but not Amy. He laughed, couldn't help himself. She spun to face him and he winced as her flashlight found his face and blinded him.

"What is it with you flashlight people and the eyes?"

"You're bleeding!"

"You should see the other guys."

"You were here?"

"I couldn't sleep, I saw someone inside…." He felt ridiculously transparent, as though she need only look at him to know he'd been forced out of his bed because he'd been having XXX-rated dreams about her.

"And so you tried to stop them? Are you *insane?*"

She moved closer, her brow furrowed with concern as she stared up into his face.

"In my defence, I did call the cops first. Senior Constable Wentworth can back me up on that."

He glanced toward the other man, but a second policeman had joined him and the two were conferring off to one side.

Amy lifted a hand and touched his jaw. Her fingers were cool and gentle but he still winced.

"Quinn." Her face was very pale.

"Amy, seriously I'm fi—"

"You idiot!" A small fist thumped into the middle of his chest. "What were you thinking? You could have been killed. I could have come in here and found you dead on the ground. Do you have any idea…?"

Tears spilled down her face. He reached out to comfort her but she took a step backward and half turned away from him. She lifted a shaking hand to swipe at her cheeks.

"I'm fine, Amy," he said, hating seeing her like this.

"I can't believe you could be so stupid. You've got a freaking law degree. Doesn't that mean you're supposed to have some smarts?"

"I wasn't really thinking, okay? I saw someone moving around inside… All I wanted to do was stop them from doing any damage to the Grand."

"From now on, you're not allowed out without adult supervision, okay?"

"Yes, Boss Lady."

He'd been hoping to squeeze a smile out of her, but she only stared at him for a long moment before looking away.

"I've got a first-aid kit in the car. Wait here," she said.

"Ames, honestly, it's a little cut, no big deal. I'm more worried about this paint. We want to mop it up before it dries, right? Because then it becomes a whole other problem."

"I've got it covered, don't worry about it."

"Amy—"

"Don't piss me off right now, Quinn. I'm so….angry with you, I don't know what I'll do."

He held up his hands, took a step back. "Okay. Fair enough."

"Wait here."

She swiveled on her heel and strode for the door. He talked to the cops while he waited, learning they suspected the vandals had had a car waiting the next street over, ready to make a quick getaway. They'd put out an all-points bulletin for any vehicles in the area acting suspiciously, but Quinn could tell they weren't holding their breath. It wasn't as though there were a million patrol cars cruising the Victorian countryside at this time of night.

His head was starting to throb when Amy returned with a professional-looking first-aid kit. She wasn't alone. A middle-aged woman and a tall, thin guy in his early twenties were following her, both carrying powerful battery-operated lanterns. He recognized them both from their visit to the hardware store earlier in the day. Like Amy, they looked as though they'd just rolled out of bed.

"This is Cheryl and Eric," Amy said as she dropped the first-aid box by his side.

They'd barely exchanged muted greetings before more people started arriving. Amy's father and mother, half a dozen other people.

"From the store," Amy explained briefly.

She went over to confer with her father, then came back to him and picked up the first-aid kit.

"Can I borrow your lantern?" she asked Cheryl.

The other woman handed the light over and Amy jerked her head, indicating Quinn should follow her.

"We'll only be in the way in here."

She led him around the edge of the spill. His side hurt when he moved and he pressed his palm against his ribs, wondering if maybe he'd cracked one or two.

The lantern cast a golden circle as they entered the foyer. Amy pointed at the steps to the balcony. "Sit."

"Seriously, Ames, it looks worse than it is. I'm more worried about the paint."

"Sit."

He did, wincing as his ribs protested.

Amy's eyes narrowed. "Have I mentioned that you're an idiot?"

"I believe you have."

"Well. You are. A big one."

She placed the lantern beside him on the step and knelt in front of him.

"What are we doing about the paint?"

"Sand. Kenny's bringing over a load from the store right now. It'll soak up the liquid. We shovel the sand into wheelbarrows and ship it out, then mop up anything that's left."

He eyed her with new respect. "You organized all this in the time it took you to get over here?" he asked.

She shrugged. "We've had spills at the store before."

Nothing as big, though, he guessed.

She stood, a bottle of alcohol solution in one hand, cotton pad in the other. "I want to clean up that cut first, make sure you don't need stitches."

He didn't say anything because he figured it was pointless. She was worried about him and if it made her feel better to clean up a scratch or two, he'd suck it up.

"It might sting a little. Try not to squeal too much," she said as she moved closer.

"Thank you for your high opinion of my manliness."

She tilted the bottle to douse the cotton in alcohol, then put the bottle down on the step. "Stay still."

She leaned forward, her free hand sliding into his hair to hold it away from his face as she gently dabbed at his cheek and temple. He stared at her face, so very close to his own. His gaze zeroed in on her lower lip. It was pale pink and looked very soft.

Very feminine. Very kissable.

This was the problem with having dirty dreams. They planted ideas in your head that had no business being there.

He averted his eyes before his thoughts went somewhere they shouldn't. Which was when he realized that he could see straight down the front of Amy's gaping pajama top.

And she wasn't wearing a bra.

He blinked, slowly.

Of course she wasn't wearing a bra. She'd jumped out of bed and into her clothes and organized a massive cleanup, all in the space of ten minutes. There'd been no time for foundation garments.

He told himself to be a gentleman but he was too busy taking in the smooth creaminess of her breasts to listen. Her nipples were pale pink, her breasts small and perky. They swayed slightly as she shifted her weight and leaned forward to inspect his scalp. Heat from her body enveloped him and he inhaled the smell of sunshine and warm skin. She was so firm, so round. He could almost feel the weight of her in his hands.

"Yow!" He jerked his head away from the fiery heat attacking his scalp and glared at Amy.

She looked utterly unrepentant. "You've got a cut on your scalp."

"No shit."

"Stop being such a wuss." She leaned forward again but he caught her arm.

"Give that stuff to me. I'll do it." Anything to end this torturous proximity.

"You won't be able to see it. It's right over the back."

She pulled her arm free and placed her left hand on his shoulder to brace herself as she leaned forward. She was standing on her toes now and her breasts were almost in his face, scant inches from his mouth. He closed his eyes, but he could still see her in his mind's eye. Pink. Plump. Firm.

Bloody hell.

If she glanced down, she was going to see exactly what she was doing to him. She was going to know he was hard for her, and then he was going to have to find some explanation that didn't involve him admitting to long-buried sexual fantasies involving her curvy body.

She leaned closer and for the fraction of a second her breast grazed his face. He opened his mouth. Couldn't help himself. Imagined himself reaching up and tugging her near while he pulled her nipple, pajama top and all, into his mouth. Actually lifted his hands, ready to slide them over her hips.

She stepped backward, bloodied cotton in hand, a frown on her face.

"I don't think you need stitches but I'm pretty sure I read somewhere that cuts on the scalp get infected really easily. I wonder if I should trim the hair around the area?"

He could just imagine how long that would take, how hard he'd be by then.

"I'm fine," he said, shooting to his feet, one hand tugging on the bottom of his T-shirt to ensure it was covering the bulge in his jeans. He'd forgotten his ribs and he grunted as pain shot up his side.

"What's wrong?"

"Nothing."

"Quinn, so help me—"

Before he could stop her, she reached out and pulled his T-shirt up, exposing his right side.

"Oh, Quinn…"

For a second he wasn't sure if her dismay was because of his injury or because she'd finally noticed his hard-on. Then she reached out and gently traced the purple marks bruising his rib cage.

He hissed in a breath, but not because it hurt. Having her touch him when he'd dreamed about touching her was a special form of torture. The kind reserved for idiots who were in danger of letting their libido ruin their lives.

"Did someone kick you? Is that the toe of a boot I can see here?" Amy asked, her expression horrified as she traced a mark above his hip. She laid her palm over the spot and stared at him, her face pale. "You really could have died, you know that?"

The fear and love in her eyes took his breath away. Shame washed over him like a bucket of cold water. While he was standing here wrestling with lust, she was worrying about him, feeling his pain.

Being his friend.

"I'm okay," he said gruffly.

She ducked her head for a few seconds. Sniffed loudly. Then nodded. "Okay." She let his T-shirt fall and moved away from him.

He stared at her downturned head. Thirty years of friendship, of platonic hugs and kisses, and it had come down to this.

To say he was confused was an understatement. Minutes ago he'd nearly done something irretrievable. He'd nearly laid hands on his best friend with sexual intent. He'd nearly changed the dynamics of their relationship forever.

Maybe it's the knock on the head.

But he knew it wasn't. It was more than that. And he had no idea how to stop it or control it. No idea at all.

AMY FOUGHT TO STOP HERSELF from touching Quinn again. Every time she relived the moment when she'd first seen his face, the blood on his forehead and cheek, the ugly red mark on his jaw, her knees got wobbly and she had to quell the urge to burst into pathetic, girly tears all over again.

She could have lost him. One of the vandals could have had a knife, or Quinn could have landed the wrong way or hit his head too hard.... He could have been gone, and she would never have heard his voice again, never looked into his dark eyes and handsome face....

She knelt over the first-aid kit, concentrating on packing away the supplies, forcing herself to get a grip.

Quinn was not dead. A little bruised, a little bloody, yes. But not dead. She was freaking out, and she needed to reel herself in before she said or did something irretrievably revealing.

"You should go back to the apartment and rest," she said, not looking up. "There are more than enough people here to help with the cleanup."

Quinn didn't say anything and she finally lifted her head to look at him. He had a small smile on his lips, a wry expression in his eyes.

Right. As if he was going to leave before things were put right.

Typical.

She opened her mouth but he beat her to it.

"I know. I'm an idiot. I can live with that."

He held out a hand. She took it and he drew her to her feet.

"This wasn't kids fooling around, Ames. You know that, right?"

"Yes."

"They were here to cause as much damage as possible, as quickly as possible."

She met his eyes. "You think it's Ulrich?"

The moment she'd seen the scale of the damage she'd known this was no ordinary act of vandalism.

"You got anyone else gunning for you at the moment I should know about? Anyone else who wants you to fail?"

"No."

"Then yes, I think it's Barry Ulrich."

Even though it was exactly what she'd expected him to say, even though she'd already concluded as much herself, she had a sudden, very inappropriate urge to laugh. It seemed so off the planet. Surreal. Someone was targeting her, trying to intimidate her into abandoning her dream of restoring the Grand. Here, in sleepy old Daylesford.

"This is nuts."

"Yeah. But at the end of the day, money is money, whether it's in the big city or out here. Ulrich stands to make a huge profit on this place if he can get it at the right price. He probably figures a little quiet sabotage will get him back in the driver's seat on this deal."

"I would rather give this place away than sell it to him, now more than ever."

Quinn smiled, his eyes crinkling at the corners. "I love it when you get all feisty."

She rolled her eyes. "You're the one with a lump the size of an egg on the back of your head because you decided to play hero. I think that officially makes you the feisty one."

Quinn picked up the first-aid kit and headed for the archway to the theatre.

"I prefer bold, if you don't mind."

"I bet you do."

He grinned at her over his shoulder and for the first time since she'd seen him all bloodied and bruised, the tight, scared feeling in her chest relaxed. He was okay. He really was.

She took a moment to absorb the realization.

Then she straightened her shoulders and lifted her chin.

There was work to do. A lot of it. And the sooner she started, the sooner she'd be finished and the sooner Barry Ulrich would understand that she wasn't the kind of woman who intimidated easily.

IT TOOK FOUR HOURS and many, many wheelbarrows full of sand to clean up the spill. By the time Amy was certain they'd mopped up the last vestiges of paint it was light outside and her impromptu team of rescuers was wilting. She had blisters on her palms from wielding first a shovel then a mop, and her stomach was rumbling with hunger.

She pushed her mop over one last section of floor, then took a moment to catch her breath and scan the theatre. Her mother and father stood to one side, their faces weary. Quinn was in the far corner, still wielding a mop even though she'd tried to send him home half a dozen times. Eric and Cheryl and the other guys from the store were scraping up the last of the sand and starting to gather shovels and spades together.

These people had gotten up in the middle of the night for her. They'd raced down here and thrown themselves into the task of saving the Grand from disaster. She would never, ever be able to repay them.

For a moment she was humbled by the knowledge, but then she realized that if gratitude was all she had to offer, then she should offer it as graciously and generously and sincerely as possible.

She slipped quietly out the front door and across the street, astonishing the young guy at the bakery with her disheveled, paint-spattered appearance.

"Performance art," she said, deadpan.

"Right."

Ten minutes later she walked back into the Grand with a tray piled high with baked goods.

"Amy! You are a goddess," Eric said when he saw her.

"I've got danishes, muffins, doughnuts, coffee scrolls, croissants. Please, dig in. Breakfast is the least I owe you."

Her mother had made a trip to the hardware store sometime during the night to collect an old card table and a few packages of cookies from the staff room. Amy set her bounty down on the table and turned to face her gathered friends and family.

"But before we eat, I wanted to say a few words."

Eric groaned theatrically and clutched his stomach.

Amy smiled. "I'll be quick, I promise. I just wanted to let you all know how much I appreciate everything you've done for me and the Grand tonight. This could have been a disaster, a huge setback, but you've all helped turn it into a minor hiccup. This has been my dream since I was ten years old, and I will always remember the kindness and generosity you've all shown me tonight. From the bottom of my heart, thank you."

"Free movies for life," Eric called out with a cheeky grin.

Amy pointed her finger at him. "Done. Consider yourselves all patrons of the Grand."

A small cheer went up. Quinn joined her as the others crowded around the card table.

"Nice speech."

"Thank you."

"Probably should have run the free-movies-for-life thing past your legal adviser first."

"I can live with it."

"Pretty generous."

She looked at him. He was watching her with warm eyes.

"Have I told you lately that you rock, Amy Parker?"

As always, his approval warmed her. "Is this the head injury talking or the fatigue?"

"Both."

"That's what I thought. So now that you've proven you're both indestructible and indefatigable, do you think I might be able to convince you to leave now?"

She kept her tone light, but he was gray with tiredness. She wanted him to rest. Ideally, she wanted to personally put him to bed and fuss over him until she'd proven to herself that he was fine. Since that was never going to happen, she would settle for sending him home.

"I might be persuaded to take a shower and grab a few hours. But only if you promise to call it quits for the day, too," he said.

"What I do and what you do are two totally separate things."

He shook his head. "Uh-uh. I will not rest until you rest."

"So chivalrous. Definitely must be the head injury. But if that's what it takes to make you behave like a sensible person, so be it."

Quinn smiled tiredly. "Then you've got yourself a deal, Parker."

Half an hour later, her rescue team had gone their separate ways and the locksmith had arrived and started installing a new, reinforced door frame and security door. She grabbed Quinn by the arm and dragged him toward the front doors.

"Go get some sleep," she told him as they reached the sidewalk. She gave him a shove in the back to send him on his way.

He took a step before turning. "I'll call you later, okay?"

Amy wasn't listening. She was too busy staring over his shoulder at the man in the expensive suit climbing out of a late-model Mercedes on the other side of the street. He was carefully not looking her way, but she'd bet her last cent Barry Ulrich had come down here to gloat and admire his handiwork.

Quinn turned to follow her sight line. She took a step toward the curb. His hand shot out to grab her forearm.

"No."

She tore her gaze from Ulrich to look at Quinn. "I just want to let him know I'm not about to run away with my tail between my legs."

"You heard what the police said. Without evidence directly linking Ulrich to the men who broke into the Grand, we've got nothing but suspicion. And you don't need me to tell you that suspicion means zip in a court of law."

"So he gets off scot-free?"

"Not necessarily. We have to wait and see. And in the meantime you can't say anything to him. I want you to promise me you won't."

She tried to pull her arm from his grasp but he was too strong.

"Could you let me go, please?" she said through gritted teeth.

"Not until you promise me you'll let me handle this."

"Believe it or not, before you came flying into town with your cape billowing, I managed fine on my own. I don't need a babysitter, and I certainly don't need a keeper."

"Fine." He let her go but didn't walk away. "Just so you know, guys like Ulrich love a fight. You take it up to him, he'll use it against you and come back at you ten times harder."

She crossed her arms over her chest. "So I should cower in the corner and thank my lucky stars he didn't set the Grand on fire. Is that what you're suggesting?"

"Play it smart. Be patient. Let the cops investigate."

She knew he was right. She wouldn't get anything except satisfaction out of taking a shot at Ulrich. But still…

She let her breath out on a noisy sigh. "Okay. Fine. You win. I promise not to say anything to him."

She knew she sounded like a sulky kid but the tight look around Quinn's mouth relaxed.

"Good choice."

She rolled her eyes. "Spare me your approval, Sir Galahad. And good night."

She strode back into the Grand, leaving him standing on the sidewalk. She knew she was taking her temper out on the wrong person, but she hated the thought that Ulrich might get away with what he'd done.

It wasn't until she'd locked the front doors behind her and slipped out past the locksmith that she remembered she'd promised to take the tray back to the bakery after she was finished with it.

"Damn it."

Sighing, she swiveled on her heel. There was a single muffin left and she took a bite out of it as she crossed the street, tray in hand. Apple and cinnamon. Not her favorite, but it would do.

The guys in the bakery were busy with the morning rush and she left the tray on the counter after making eye contact with one of them and mouthing her thanks. A great wave of weariness swept over her as she turned to go. She needed to get some sleep.

She saw Ulrich the moment she stepped onto the sidewalk. He was standing a few paces away with a guy she recognized as his foreman. They were facing the Grand and Ulrich was sketching shapes in the air with his hands, pointing to the windows, the roofline. His foreman was making notes on a notebook, nodding his head.

As though Ulrich owned the Grand and his foreman was making plans to bring Ulrich's vision to life.

Not. Freaking. Likely.

Not in her lifetime.

Anger born of outrage and fear rose up inside her. She didn't stop to think, just strode across to block their view.

"What do you think you're doing?" she asked.

Barry looked startled for a few seconds, then a patronizing smile curled his lips.

"Ms. Parker. Allow me to offer my sympathies. I hear you've had a bit of a rough time overnight."

She narrowed her eyes. "Yes, and don't think I don't know who's responsible for that, asshole."

The smile dropped from Ulrich's face. His pale blue eyes grew hard. "I know you're not familiar with business and the way professionals usually conduct themselves, so I'm going to give you a tip, Ms. Parker. Watch your mouth."

"Why, asshole? Because if I don't you'll hire some-one else to vandalize the Grand? Is that what you're saying, asshole?"

Ulrich's nostrils flared. "I'd be very careful what kind of accusations I threw around if I were you."

"If I were you, I'd remember who owns the Grand. *Asshole.*"

Suddenly Ulrich was in her face, breathing bad coffee breath on her, so close she could see where he'd missed a few whiskers when he shaved this morning.

"Listen up, little girl. I don't need to lift a finger to en-sure you'll fail because you'll do that all on your own. If you'd had half a brain, you would have taken my offer while you had the chance. Now you're going to lose ev-erything. I almost feel sorry for you."

He stared into her eyes for a long moment, then turned away.

"Come on, Brian," he said to his foreman, not even looking at the other man as he walked away.

Her hands were shaking. No use pretending they weren't. Barry Ulrich was one scary, angry bastard. She watched him walk away, feeling very small and impotent and vulnerable.

"Hey, Barry!" she called after him.

He glanced over his shoulder impatiently. Amy wound back her arm, took aim and threw in one smooth move. The muffin hit him dead center of the forehead before crumbling down the front of his expensive suit.

He blinked, his mouth open, utterly stunned. A tide of crimson color washed up his neck and into his face. She made a big show of dusting her hands together and turning her back on him. Despite the bravado her heart was banging against her rib cage.

Shit.

He looked so angry. Almost psychotic.

She crossed the street to the Grand, resisting the urge to break into a run, expecting to feel a hand on her shoulder with every step.

She'd grabbed the tiger by the tail and given it a big old yank and any minute now the tiger was going to pounce on her and rip her head off.

It wasn't until she was in the Grand and the doors locked that she felt safe enough to look back across the street.

Ulrich was on the phone. One hand dusted muffin crumbs off the front of his suit as he spoke, his dead, flat eyes fixed on her.

The reality of what she'd done sunk in.

Quinn was going to kill her.

IT WASN'T UNTIL he got back to the apartment that Quinn remembered he'd planned to check out that morning and move into his parents' place. He was so tired that for a few minutes he contemplated booking in for another night just so he could crawl straight into bed. Then he told himself to man up and went to his room to pack. It didn't take long and within fifteen minutes he was at the front desk handing over his credit card.

Familiar smells rushed at him when he opened the
door to his old family home. His mother's homemade pot-
pourri, his father's pipe tobacco, furniture polish. The
place was dark and he dumped his overnight bag in the
hall and did a quick lap of the house, opening curtains and
blinds as he went. He pushed open his old bedroom door
last and stood in the doorway staring at his single bed and
the various movie and sports posters covering his walls.

Hello, 1997.

He crossed to the window and pulled the curtains
wide. Outside, the straggly privet hedge still struggled to
create a privacy barrier between this house and the
Parkers' next door. He stared at Amy's old bedroom
window, facing his across the way.

He'd almost done something really stupid today. If
Amy hadn't stepped back when she did…

He unlocked the window and gave the frame a thump
with his closed fist before attempting to push it up. It
stuck for a moment, then gave in a rush. Cool air flowed
into the room as he pushed the window all the way open.

He breathed in the smell of wet earth and green things.
Maybe this…*thing* he had for Amy was a reaction to
being back home again after all these years. An X-rated
form of nostalgia.

Or maybe he'd never quite gotten over the crush he'd
had all those years ago, and it was only now that he was
getting a divorce that he was allowing himself to acknowledge the attraction again.

Or maybe he simply needed to grab a good night's
sleep and wake up with some much-needed perspective.
Because at the end of the day, if it came down to a battle
between short-term lust and long-term friendship, friendship was the winner every time. Right?

Right?

He returned to the entrance hall to get his bag then grabbed some sheets from the hall cupboard to make up his bed. He hadn't slept in a single bed since he'd left home. He wasn't looking forward to reliving the experience.

He took a few minutes to examine his injuries in the bathroom mirror before he showered. The bruise on his face wasn't as bad as he'd thought and while his ribs were sore, they weren't overly painful. Not cracked, then, he figured.

He showered quickly, then walked naked back into his old bedroom. His bed sagged in the middle as it took his weight. He rolled onto his side and closed his eyes.

A few hours of shut-eye and the world would right itself.

A great theory, but as he drifted toward sleep, images from the day slipped into his unguarded mind. He saw Amy's eyes staring into his, full of trust and concern. He smelled her warm, soft scent. He remembered the pink of her nipples. Felt again the press of her hands on his body.

The problem with lusting after someone you'd known for years was that it was hard to separate the lust from the liking and the love that had always been there.

He tried hard to remember why that was such a bad thing as sleep finally took him.

CHAPTER SEVEN

"Hey."

Amy nearly dropped the putty knife she was holding as she whirled to face Quinn the next morning.

He gave her a quizzical look. "Sorry. Didn't mean to startle you."

Despite the bruise on his jaw, he looked delicious in worn jeans and a dark gray T-shirt. Her heart did its usual little kick-skip before resuming normal duties.

"I'm good. Just not expecting you."

He checked his watch. "It's right on eight."

"Sure. I meant I didn't hear you. That's all." She gave him an overly bright smile. "How are you feeling?"

"Nothing that won't heal."

The guilt and anxiety she'd been experiencing ever since she lobbed the muffin at Ulrich tightened around her chest. She should have called Quinn yesterday and told him what she'd done. But she hadn't, and she'd been living in fear of someone else telling him ever since. Every time the phone had rung last night she'd flinched, anticipating a blistering lecture from him for her stupid, impulsive act. But he hadn't called, because clearly he hadn't heard yet, despite the fact that there had been several witnesses to her muffin assault and gossip was practically one of the five food groups in Daylesford.

So tell him now. Tell him right now before he hears it from someone else.

She opened her mouth, but no words came out.

If there was one thing she'd never been able to stand, it had been Quinn's disapproval. Worse still, his disappointment. He'd warned her. Told her not to approach Ulrich. But she'd let her emotions override her.

"We should get started. Dad's going to deliver more primer this afternoon and I figure if we go hard we can probably get most of the cracks and holes filled today," she said.

Quinn was still watching her as though he was trying to work something out. She was such a crap liar. Always had been.

"You sure you're okay?" he asked.

"Absolutely. Just keen to get stuck into it, that's all. Make sure we don't let Ulrich put us off schedule."

She turned and grabbed a bucket of premixed spackling compound before he could ask any more questions.

"Might as well do what we did the other day," she said. "I'll handle the foyer and balcony while you do down here. The scaffolding should arrive some time this afternoon, so that should make things a lot easier for you, save you moving the ladder around as much."

She didn't look back at him as she headed for the foyer. Once she was out of sight she stopped and smacked herself on the forehead with her open palm. Seriously, what did she think she was going to achieve, putting off telling him what she'd done?

There's always a chance Ulrich will let it slide, a little voice volunteered in the back of her mind. *Then Quinn won't have to know how stupid you were.* It was the weasel voice again, telling her what she most wanted to hear, and she knew better than to trust it.

And yet…

It was possible that Ulrich was so embarrassed about being assaulted by a woman armed with a bakery product that he'd let the whole thing slide. He was a short man, after all, and often short men were overly concerned with appearances and status.

That's right, Amy, that's the kind of guy he is—a wimp who's more concerned with his dignity than winning. Not.

She pried the lid off the spackle bucket. She was simply going to have to wait Ulrich out, see what he did with the advantage she'd given him. Have her charged with assault, perhaps. Or maybe there was some other way he could use her impetuous act against her—not being a sneaky, underhanded lowlife, she wasn't well-versed in these matters.

But before any of that happened, she'd tell Quinn. Definitely. Before lunch. Or at the very latest by the end of the day. Although maybe it would be best to take him out for dinner first, get him a little mellow with wine before confessing all.

She was still pondering how best to broach the subject when there was a knock on the front door around midday.

She was up the ladder in the balcony filling a large crack and she shouted down to Quinn, asking him if he was free to get it.

"Sure," he hollered back.

She pressed spackle into the jagged crack, being careful not to overfill it so that it would be easy to sand back tomorrow. She was knifing up a fresh bladeful when she heard Quinn's footsteps on the stairs.

"Who was it?" she asked.

Quinn didn't immediately answer and she glanced over her shoulder to see him standing at the foot of the ladder, an official-looking envelope in hand.

"What's up?" she asked.

"Registered letter. From Ulrich's lawyers."

The blood rushed from her head.

Suddenly she wished she'd been brave enough to tell Quinn everything this morning. Hell, she should have called him the moment she'd realized how dumb she'd been. Maybe then they could have come up with some plan to neutralize whatever lay within that envelope.

Because there was no doubt in her mind that there was something unpleasant waiting to be unleashed from within that innocuous-looking piece of office stationery.

She forced her stiff arms and legs to descend the ladder. Then she put down the putty knife and bucket of filler and reached out to take the envelope from Quinn.

"It's probably another offer to buy the Grand," he said reassuringly. "At a bargain price, naturally, now that you've been bullied into submission."

She slipped her thumb beneath the flap and broke the seal. There was a many-paged document inside. She unfolded it and read the first page.

"What's he offering?" Quinn asked.

Amy closed her eyes for a long beat. Quinn had warned her, after all. *Ten times harder.*

"Amy, what's going on?"

She opened her eyes. Looked at Quinn. Took a deep breath. "He's suing me for defamation."

Quinn looked taken aback. "What the hell?"

He plucked the papers from her hands and scanned them quickly.

"It says here there was an incident on the morning of the twenty-eighth of April. That's yesterday. He's got a list of witnesses—" His gaze lifted to her face. "What did you do?" His voice was very low and flat.

She swallowed noisily. "I screwed up. I didn't mean to, but I did. He was just so arrogant. I wanted him to know I wasn't scared of him. But he knew I was. I could hardly stop my hands from shaking."

"What happened?"

"He was standing in front of the Grand, talking to his foreman, dictating notes on stuff he wanted to do. You know, once the place was his. It just really… I saw red. So I asked him what he was doing, and he offered me his sympathy. Can you believe that?"

"Tell me the rest."

"I told him that I knew he was the one who was responsible for me having a hard time. And I called him an asshole."

Her stomach was churning and she'd started to sweat.

"He told me to watch my mouth, so I called him an asshole a few more times and asked if he was threatening to hire someone else to vandalize the place. Then he got in my face and told me I was going to fail and how happy that was going to make him."

She wiped her damp hands down the front of her jeans.

"Is there anything else I should know?" Quinn asked.

"I threw a muffin at him."

"A muffin."

"Yes. Apple and cinnamon. It was in my hand, and he'd scared me so much. I just… I called out, and he turned around. And I threw it at him."

Quinn's face was utterly impassive. "Where did it hit him?"

She touched herself on the forehead. A muscle flexed in Quinn's jaw.

"I was going to tell you. Tonight. Over a nice bottle of wine."

He stared at her for a long moment. Then he reread the cover letter and flicked through the attached pages. He looked grim. And furious.

"Am I in big trouble?" she asked.

"Let's see. You accosted a well-known local business-man in the street and publicly accused him of hiring criminals to vandalize your property. You insulted him. Then you threw a missile at his head. What do you think?"

"Maybe if I apologized…?" It might be enough to appease Ulrich. It would be hard to make herself sound sincere, but she'd do it for the Grand.

"He doesn't want your apology, Amy. He wants to break you. He wants to suck your bank account dry so you have no choice but to sell him the Grand. There's no way he's going to accept an apology. He will play this out till it ends up in court and you're charged with every legal fee and damage he can throw your way."

She stared into Quinn's angry face. He wasn't exag-gerating. He was simply telling her what she had sus-pected the moment she calmed down enough to realize what she'd done. She'd screwed up. Big time.

"Why do you think I told you to stay away from him? Did you need me to spell it out to you? I told you he was the kind of guy who'd use anything you did against him. And still you went out and handed him your own head on a silver platter."

Quinn threw the letter away as though he couldn't bear to look at it a moment longer.

"You should have just given him the keys to the Grand. Saved yourself a few years and thousands of dollars."

He had more to say, but it faded to white noise as the full reality sunk in. A huge wave of dizziness hit her. In all the years of saving and bargaining and scheming to make the Grand hers, she'd never doubted that she would succeed. She'd simply refused to accept that it would be any other way. She'd been unshakable.

But she couldn't see a way out now. Even if Quinn agreed to represent her for free, there would be court costs and other expenses. By the time Ulrich had finished with her, she'd be broke. And she would lose the Grand.

The edges of her vision went blurry. She was in real danger of passing out. How very damsel-in-distress of her.

She bent her knees, stretching out a hand to find the floor as it rose up to meet her. She landed on her ass with a thump. Her knees came up instinctively and she put her head between her legs, panting as though she'd run a race.

"Amy." Quinn's voice seemed to come from very far away.

She couldn't get enough air, even though she was breathing like a bellows.

"Amy, calm down. It'll be okay."

He was on his knees beside her, a concerned look on his face.

It wasn't going to be okay. She could see it all now, Ulrich smiling smugly as she signed the papers to give him the Grand, could practically hear the wrecking ball smashing into the building.

"I'm sorry for yelling," Quinn said. "I freaked out for a moment, but we're good. We'll work this out, okay?"

She shook her head. Tried to explain despite the fact she was hyperventilating. "You're right...should have kept my mouth shut…wanted to prove…I wasn't afraid. Just…shot myself in the foot."

Quinn put his hands on her shoulders and gave her a gentle shake.

"Listen to me. We can fix this." She shook her head again and he squeezed her shoulders. "We can, Amy. We'll find a way. I promise. You won't lose the Grand. I never should have said that."

Her breathing slowed. She peered up at him, wanting to believe him so badly but desperately afraid of the future she'd seen laid out before her.

He held her gaze, his own absolutely steady and certain. "Have I ever let you down, Ames?"

She stared at him, their faces a few feet apart. The only time Quinn had ever disappointed her was when he'd chosen Lisa instead of her. And she'd never blamed him for that. He was the best friend a person could have, bar none. A man in a million.

And she'd tried to excise him from her life because she couldn't get over her own jealousy and frustration.

Her eyes widened. For a moment she was stunned as the full enormity of her own stupidity and selfishness hit her. She'd almost pushed this good, loving, amazing man out of her life.

She made an inarticulate noise. Fueled by guilt and regret and love and gratitude, she launched herself at him. Her body hit his with enough force to make him grunt as she flung her arms around his neck, her face finding his shoulder. For a moment they teetered off balance, then her momentum tipped him over. He landed on his back, her arms still clamped around his neck, her body sprawled on top of his.

"I'm sorry," she said, her words muffled by his T-shirt.

"You deserve so much better. I'm so sorry. I've been so stupid. So bloody stupid."

Their legs were tangled, her breasts flattened against his chest. One of Quinn's hands warmed the middle of her back, the other found the nape of her neck.

"Ames, you don't need to apologize to me. Like I said, we'll work this out. Ulrich is trying to scare you, and I shouldn't have let him get to me."

He didn't understand. Had no idea what she'd tried to do.

"I don't deserve you," she said. "You've always been such a good friend to me."

"You've been a good friend to me, too, Ames. The best."

His deep voice vibrated through her with every word. She could feel his chest rising and falling with each breath. She lifted her head to look into his eyes. He looked back at her, a small, sweet smile curving his lips.

"You're my bud. Always were, always will be."

She could see all the tiny individual bristles of his beard. His eyes were very dark, rich as bittersweet chocolate. His mouth was mere inches from hers, his breath fanning her face. For the first time she fully registered the fact that she was lying on top of him, hip to hip, chest to chest.

Like a lover.

She could feel the hard, hot resilience of his body beneath hers, could smell his skin, his aftershave. Awareness flooded her, sending heat up into her face and down between her thighs.

She hadn't been this close to him for years. Not since they were kids.

Suddenly her heart was pounding for an entirely different reason. Her gaze dropped to his mouth.

If ever there was a moment of temptation, this was it.

If ever she was going to press her lips to his, touch him, move her body against his in the way that she'd dreamed so many, many times, this was it. All she had to do was close the small distance between them and lower her mouth to his. Kiss him. Run her tongue over his lips. Taste him. Give in to sixteen years of desire and need.

You're my bud. Always were, always will be.

His words echoed in her mind and she forced herself to listen to them, absorb them. If she kissed Quinn, there was a very good chance that he would be appalled. Shocked. Embarrassed.

It was enough to make her start to withdraw. Then she remembered the discussion she'd had with her mother last night.

Some smart woman will snap him up. And it won't take long, either.

"Ames?" Quinn's mouth curled into a curious half smile.

She took a shaky breath. Was she really going to let him slip through her fingers a second time? Was she really prepared to love him from afar for years and never, ever take a chance? Even if that chance carried with it an enormous risk of rejection and loss?

He was lying beneath her right now, six foot plus of hard, warm male. And she was sick of not knowing. Of wanting and not having.

It was now or never.

Now.

Or never.

Her heart pounding, Amy closed her eyes.

Then she lowered her head and kissed her best friend.

QUINN'S HEART SLAMMED against his rib cage as Amy's mouth pressed against his. For a crazy second he didn't know what was happening, then her tongue grazed his lower lip and a shiver of pure need tightened his body.

His instinctive response was to open his mouth and kiss her back. Slide his tongue along hers, taste her. Pull her body closer. But this was Amy.

Amy, for God's sake.

His hands found her shoulders, but he didn't know what to do. Push her away? Pull her closer?

Then suddenly she was gone, rolling away from him. She landed on her belly beside him, her face pressed into her hands.

What the hell had just happened?

"Ames…?"

He reached out to lay a hand on her shoulder. She tensed. A long moment passed. Then her shoulders lifted beneath his hand as she took a deep breath.

"I'm sorry. I don't know— I didn't mean for that to happen," she said, her voice so choked it was almost inaudible.

"Amy. Talk to me. What's going on?"

"Nothing. That was…dumb." She shook her head. "Let's just pretend this never happened."

He laughed, even though he was far from amused. He'd spent the last few days feeling like a sick puppy for getting hot over his best friend, and now she wanted him to forget she'd kissed him?

"Not likely, Ames."

She started to scramble to her feet but he sat up and caught her arm.

"Hang on a minute. You can't stick your tongue down my throat then make a run for it."

She crouched awkwardly beside him, anchored by his hand on her arm. Her face was averted, her gaze fixed on the floor as though she was afraid to look at him.

"It was a mistake."

Maybe. Almost definitely. But he still needed to know why it had happened. Why now, after all these years?

He caught her chin with his free hand, forcing her to make eye contact with him.

"Why?"

"You're a smart guy. Work it out."

"I don't want to guess. I want to know."

The look she gave him was tortured. "Please…"

Part of him felt like an ass for forcing an answer from her, but his gut told him this was important. Vital, even.

"Tell me."

Her jaw muscle flexed beneath his hand. She closed her eyes for a long beat. Then she opened them and looked straight into his eyes.

"Haven't you ever wondered what it would be like? The two of us, together?"

He stared at her. For a moment his mind was a perfect blank.

Color flooded Amy's face. He could feel the embarrassed heat of it beneath his fingers.

"See? I told you it was dumb."

She tried to pull away from him again but he didn't release his grip.

"Let me go. I told you—"

"Yes," he said. "The answer is yes."

She stilled. He'd shocked her. Well, she'd shocked him.

Somewhere, in the back of his brain, a voice was screaming out a warning. Something about there being no turning back from this moment.

He could barely hear it over the thumping of his heart. Amy was attracted to him. She'd thought about the two of them together. Skin to skin. Him inside her.

His gaze dropped to her mouth. How many times had he studied it over the past few days? Wondered what she would taste like, how she would feel? How many times had he dreamed about her in that long-ago summer when they were both fourteen?

He stroked his fingers along the delicate line of her jaw.

"Amy," he said, his voice very low.

She made a small sound in the back of her throat. He slid his hand around to palm the nape of her neck. Her gaze dropped to his mouth.

Time slowed as he pulled her gently toward him.

Her lips parted.

Then his lips were on hers. Moving over them, learning the shape of her, the feel of her. Soft and full. Silk and velvet. She opened her mouth to him and their tongues touched for the first time. She tasted good, sweet and hot.

He wanted more. Much more. He drove his fingers into the hair at the base of her skull and held her head in the palm of his hand as he explored her mouth with his. Her hands found his chest, clutching his T-shirt, the fabric biting into the back of his neck as she dragged him closer.

Closer was good. Closer was what he wanted, too. He spread his free hand on her hip, pulling her down with him as he sank to the floor. A wave of pure heat rolled through him as her weight settled over him. He slid his hand onto the roundness of her backside, his fingers curving to her shape as he pulled her against the hardness of his erection.

"Quinn," she breathed, her hips circling against him.

His hands were shaking as he found the waistband of her sweater. He wanted so much, needed so much, he didn't know where to begin. He smoothed his palm up her warm belly. He cupped her breast, his thumb brushing over her nipple through the silk of her bra. She quivered like a plucked guitar string, her breath coming in desperate little pants.

He rolled so that she was beneath him, ignoring the ache of protest from his bruised ribs. He was so far beyond pain it wasn't funny. She spread her legs to create a cradle for his hips and he lost his mind for a minute as he pressed his hard-on into the heated juncture of her thighs.

He reached for the hem of her sweater and pushed it up over her breasts, then shoved her bra up, too, finesse be damned. She was a study in pink and cream, so pretty and sexy it hurt to look at her.

"Beautiful," he murmured, then he lowered his head and pulled one of her pouty little nipples into his mouth.

She gasped and gripped his shoulders.

"*Quinn.*"

Her hands slid across his back, his chest, his ass. Then she was sliding a hand between their bodies and smoothing her palm up and down the swollen length of his erection through the denim of his jeans.

His breath hissed between his teeth. He wanted to be inside her. He wanted to feel her slick and firm around him. His hand found the stud on her jeans, popping it open. She lifted her hips encouragingly as he found the tab on her zipper and tugged it down. Her belly trembled as he slid his hand beneath the elastic of her panties. His fingers caressed silky hair then slid into slick heat.

His gut clenched as he felt how incredibly wet she was. He traced her intimate folds, then slid a finger inside her. She tightened around him, sexy and hot, her hips lifting off the floor as he stroked in and out of her.

"Amy."

"Hurry. Please."

He reached for his belt buckle, tugged it free. Her hands found his zipper and pulled it down. Then she was inside his underwear, stroking her hand up and down his shaft, her thumb caressing the head of his penis.

He shuddered, his whole body tensing. He started to peel her jeans away from her hips. Five more seconds and he'd be inside her, inside all that tight, wet heat, his—

"Amy? Hello?"

They both froze.

"Shit," Amy whispered.

It was her mom. They stared at each other, their bodies slick and steamy with lust. Amy was flushed, her nipples still tight and wet from his mouth. Her mouth was swollen, her eyes hazy with need.

"Amy? Is there anybody here or am I just talking to myself?"

They heard the scuff of footsteps, then the distinct sound of someone climbing the stairs.

"She's coming up here!" Amy hissed.

They rolled away from each other, Amy jerking her bra and sweater down while he struggled with his zipper and belt buckle. They'd barely scrambled to their feet when Mrs. Parker crossed the upper foyer and entered the balcony.

"THERE YOU ARE. Didn't you hear me calling?" Amy's mother asked.

Amy resisted the urge to check her fly was closed, even though she couldn't one hundred percent remember zipping it up.

"Mom. Hi. Um, no, Quinn and I were busy discussing a thing."

Her mother's gaze went from Amy to Quinn and back again.

"How are you doing, Mrs. P.?" Quinn said.

"I'm fine, thanks, Quinn. Thought I should pop in and check how things are going down here."

"Things are going well. Really well. We're getting lots done," Amy said.

She risked a glance at Quinn. His hair was mussed and his T-shirt rumpled, the fabric strategically bunched in front of his crotch. He looked as though he'd rolled out of bed. Which, in a way, he had.

I rumpled that hair. I gave him the hard-on he's hiding beneath that T-shirt.

It was almost inconceivable, and yet it had happened. Her heart was still pounding, her body still throbbing with need. Quinn had wanted her.

Quinn.

Her wildest dream come true.

Her mother shifted the strap of her handbag higher on her shoulder. "When do you think you'll be ready to paint?"

Out of the corner of her eye Amy saw Quinn stoop to collect Ulrich's letter from the floor.

"Soon. We need to finish prepping the walls. I was hoping to have it done over the next few days," Amy said.

Quinn cleared his throat. "Ames, I might leave you two to catch up for a bit. I've got some business to take care of."

His face was shuttered, utterly unreadable.

"Um, sure."

He nodded to her mother, then turned and headed for the archway to the upper foyer. She stared after him.

"Amy?"

Her mother's words jolted her focus back into the room. Amy blinked, turned to her mother.

"Sorry?"

"What's going on?"

"I told you. We're still prepping the walls."

Her mother crossed her arms over her chest. "I didn't come down in the last shower. I know what I walked in on."

"Mom, nothing's going on."

Her mother sighed heavily. "All right. Keep it to yourself. But just remember, Quinn's going through a difficult time right now."

"I know that."

"Men do strange things when they come out of long-term relationships, Amy. Whatever is *not happening* between the two of you, make sure that you're both on the same page. I'd hate to see you get hurt."

"Nothing's going on."

"Hmm. Show me how the floors came up after the spill."

Amy took her mother downstairs, watching a little impatiently as her mother inspected the floor.

"Not too bad. You might need to get into some of these cracks with a wire brush, but most of it should sand out when you do the refinishing," her mother said.

At any other time, Amy would appreciate her mother's expert opinion, but all she wanted right now was to talk to Quinn. She needed to hear his voice, to know where he was at, what he was thinking. Why he'd left the way he had.

"Well, I guess I should get back to the store."

"Okay. Thanks for dropping by." Amy was already fingering her phone in her pocket.

Amy kissed her mother goodbye and waited till her footsteps had faded before flipping her cell phone open.

If her mother hadn't arrived, she and Quinn would be lovers by now. They would have been as close as two people could get. It would have changed everything.

But her mother had arrived. And Amy was afraid that everything had changed anyway.

You don't know that. You don't know what he's feeling right now, what he's thinking.

But she kept remembering the shuttered look on his face before he'd ducked and run for cover. Not exactly inspiring stuff.

She pressed speed dial and waited for him to pick up. His phone went straight to voice mail. She tried his parents' place, but the phone simply rang out. Then she tried his cell again, and again she got voice mail.

Finally she closed her phone.

He didn't want to talk to her.

It might not mean anything, Weasel piped up.

But she knew Weasel was wrong. As always.

CHAPTER EIGHT

QUINN HAD NO IDEA how things had gotten so crazy so quickly. Sure, he'd been thinking about Amy a lot over the last few days. Remembering feelings long forgotten. And there'd been that dream and her gaping pajama top…

But the moment he'd touched her, tasted her, felt her touching him… He'd lost it. Pure and simple. He'd felt as desperate and urgent and clumsy as the horny teen he'd once been.

He took a mouthful of beer. He was sitting on the back deck of his parents' house. Had been ever since he bailed on Amy.

She probably thought he was a shameless opportunist. And if she didn't, she should. She was his best friend. So what if she'd admitted to being curious about what it would be like to get naked with him? Since when did that signal a free-for-all? If her mother hadn't arrived, he would have taken her right there on the bare boards of the balcony.

You have to apologize. You have to look her in the eye and apologize.

He checked his watch. He'd been gone a couple of hours. He should go back to the Grand right now. Talk to Amy. Say what needed to be said.

He didn't move. Didn't so much as flex a muscle.

He was thirty years old, and on the verge of divorce. Was it just him, or was it a really lousy time for him to start obsessing over his best friend?

He squinted his eyes against the weak winter sun, trying to sort things out in his mind.

Amy was his dearest and oldest friend.

He valued his relationship with her. Had even felt compelled to drop the L-word on her recently, despite both of them having left the sentiment unspoken for years.

And he wanted to sleep with her, and had almost done so, despite all of the above.

He had no idea what Amy wanted from him. Friendship, yes. Sex? A couple of hours ago, yes. But now that she'd had time to think things over? He had no idea.

Worse, he had no idea what *he* wanted, beyond the obvious. He'd been with Lisa for nearly fifteen years, married to her for six of them. There had been other girlfriends in high school when he and Lisa had broken up a couple of times. There had been a six-month break when they were at university when they'd both seen other people. But other than those few periods in his life, he had always been one half of a whole. Quinn and Lisa, Lisa and Quinn. Now, after nearly a year on his own, he was starting to understand that he'd lost himself in his marriage. Been subsumed by Lisa's ambition and drive, allowed her needs and wants to swamp his own.

He'd lost track of the things he considered important. A career he could believe in, a family of his own, involvement in the community, personal fulfillment. He had no idea how to bring those things back into focus for himself again, where to start.

All of which meant he had no business fooling around

with Amy. What did he have to offer her, after all? His life crisis? His confusion and frustration and bitterness? She deserved a hell of a lot more than that from him.

He smiled grimly at his own arrogance. He could almost hear Amy in his head: *Who says I want anything from you, buddy?* He was being hugely presumptuous, making assumptions about what he thought she might want.

He needed to talk to her. They were both adults, after all. They knew each other well, respected each other. Cared deeply for one another. There was no reason why they couldn't sit down and discuss what had almost happened between them.

He pushed himself to his feet and dusted off the butt of his jeans. Then he drank the last of his beer and went to talk to Amy.

AMY WAS TESTING the stability of the newly-erected scaffolding when the back of her neck prickled. She knew without looking that Quinn had returned.

He'd been gone three hours. Not a good sign. Definitely not the sign of a man who had suddenly realized that he was in love with his best friend.

As if that was ever going to happen.

She took a moment to compose herself, then glanced over her shoulder. "Hey."

"Hey."

He was standing in the center of the cinema, hands in the back pockets of his jeans. He was trying to look casual, but she could see the tension in his shoulders.

Her stomach dipped in dismay. This was going to be bad.

"The scaffolding guys came," she said, patting one of the uprights. Anything to hold off the conversation she knew was coming.

"Should make life a bit easier," he said.

"Definitely."

An awkward silence fell.

"We should probably talk," she said at exactly the same moment he did.

They both laughed. Her gaze touched his briefly, but she was too nervous to hold it.

"Great minds think alike," he said.

"Yeah."

A heavy weight descended on her chest. She knew what he was about to say. It was in every line of his face and body. *Sorry, Ames. I have no idea what that was all about. Let's chalk it up as a bold experiment and move on.*

Or something like that. Whatever it was, however he phrased it, she knew it wasn't going to be what she wanted to hear.

Quinn didn't love her the way she loved him. She should get it tattooed on the inside of her eyelids, in case she was ever tempted to forget again.

"What happened earlier… I feel like I should…" Quinn laughed awkwardly and ran a hand through his hair. "This is a lot harder than I thought it would be. Things kind of got out of control. And I'm sorry about that."

He was sorry.

Of course he was.

"You don't need to apologize."

"I think I do. Even if we weren't best friends, there are about a million other reasons why what happened was a bad idea. I'm still sorting through all this shit with Lisa, I'm only in town for a few weeks, I have no idea how my life is going to look in a few months' time, let alone next year…" He shrugged. "I'm not exactly a great prospect right now."

She should probably thank him for not voicing the

most obvious reason why what happened was forever going to remain a freak one-off: he wasn't interested in her in that way. She was filed firmly under the heading "friend" in his mind. Always had been, always would be.

"I value your friendship too much to screw it up with sex," he said.

And there it was. The bottom line.

She straightened her spine. Time to come to the party. Help sweep this mess under the carpet and ignore it till it went away.

"I feel the same way," she said. She tried to force more past the lump in her throat but couldn't do it.

Quinn took a step toward her, his face creased with concern. "Ames."

She held up a hand to keep him at bay. Dear God, if he touched her right now she really would fall apart.

"I'm fine. Really. Just relieved that we're both on the same page. I was wigging out for a while there."

"You and me both. Kind of caught me off guard."

"Me, too," she said. "But we're both cool with it, so it's all good. Right?"

"Absolutely."

She gathered together the remnants of her pride and mustered yet another smile. "It's past three. We might as well call it quits for the day, start fresh tomorrow."

There was a short pause before Quinn responded. "Sure. I'll see you at eight tomorrow morning, okay?"

"Great. See you then."

She kept the smile on her mouth until his footsteps had faded. Then she sank onto one of the crossbars of the scaffolding.

Her chest ached. She rubbed the heel of her hand against her sternum and stared at the floor.

Could have been worse. You could have declared yourself.

Something to be grateful for. Not much, but something.

QUINN HEADED FOR the council building when he left the Grand, his hands deep in his coat pockets.

He told himself he was pleased with the way things had gone with Amy. They'd both agreed that rolling around on the floor was a mistake. That their friendship was worth more than any sexual curiosity either of them might harbor. A few days from now, it would be as though it had never happened. Business as usual.

He snorted. *You're so full of it, Whitfield.*

It was unlikely he was going to forget those few hot minutes with Amy in his arms anytime soon.

But it wasn't as though he had an alternative.

Denise looked up from the reception desk when he entered the council building.

"Quinn Whitfield. You look like you took on a football team."

He fingered his jaw. The swelling had gone down overnight, but the bruise was still a lurid purple-gray.

"Hockey team, actually. Girls' under fourteen."

Denise smiled sympathetically. "I heard about what happened. I was going to call Ames tonight to see how she was holding up. What a pack of bastards."

"You can say that again."

"Do the cops have any idea who did it?"

"Ideas, but not much evidence. Listen, Denise, what can you tell me about Ulrich Construction's relationship with council?"

Denise's heavily mascaraed eyes went wide for a

second as she joined the dots. Then she pushed her office chair toward the filing cabinet behind her desk.

"Tell me what you need," she said. She opened the file drawer and looked at him expectantly.

He smiled faintly at her ready response. "Nothing that might get you in trouble." He glanced toward the corridor leading to the inner offices.

"Don't worry about Reg. He's never here. He spends more time at the Daylesford golf course than the club pro."

"In that case, I'll take anything you've got on Ulrich Construction."

Denise started pulling files. "If it was for anyone else, I'd tell you to take a hike, but Amy is a goddess. If it wasn't for her, I'd still be lying around in my track pants, stuffing my face and feeling sorry for myself. After my divorce, she listened to me moan for a few months, then she put a rocket up me. She helped me pick a secretarial course, then convinced her dad to put me on at the hardware store so I could get some experience. A year later, I landed this job. Amy's the best."

"I know."

She carried the files she'd pulled over to the photocopier then glanced across at him.

"Do you mind double-sided copies? We're on an eco-friendly kick."

"Double-sided is fine."

He took the files home and went over them, making notes. Then he logged on to the Internet and did a bit of poking around.

He came up with an interesting picture: until five years ago, Ulrich had been very small potatoes, building only a handful of residential houses a year. Then the company suddenly landed a slew of contracts for commercial projects, many of them originating from council. A real Cinderella story.

If you were the kind of guy who believed in fairy tales.

He looked up the company's street address and grabbed his car keys. Ten minutes later he pulled up out the front of an ugly new commercial development, a series of squat concrete cubes that was all about cheap construction and precious little else. Located on the outskirts of town, it was surrounded by lots of churned-up mud and staked-out plots of land that signaled more development was slated for the future. Quinn parked across the street and climbed out of his car.

Ulrich's Mercedes was parked out the front of his offices. Quinn spared a glance for the lush leather interior as he walked past. An electronic buzzer announced his arrival as he entered a small reception area boasting a single couch, a coffee table full of building magazines and a desk with a computer and a pretty brunette.

She looked up from her keyboard and smiled. "Good afternoon. How can I help you?"

Quinn was tempted to ask if she minded handing over Ulrich's financial records but she looked too young to appreciate the joke.

"I'd like to see Mr. Ulrich. I don't have an appointment, but if you tell him I represent Amy Parker, I'm sure he'll see me."

He handed over one of his business cards. The receptionist's smile faltered at the mention of Amy and he guessed Ulrich had been talking about her around the office.

Interesting.

"If you'll just give me a moment," she said.

She disappeared down the hallway. He propped his hip against her desk and studied the photographs of various developments on the walls. More examples of the concrete box school of architecture. It was a lucky day for Daylesford when Amy beat Ulrich to the Grand. Quinn could imagine the eyesore the developer had planned to inflict on the community.

"I'm sorry, Mr. Whitfield, but Mr. Ulrich is tied up right now. He suggests you make an appointment if you'd like to see him."

To her credit, the receptionist couldn't quite look him in the eye as she lied through her teeth. Quinn straightened. He'd half expected Ulrich to be this petty and stupid.

"Thanks," he said.

He exited the building and crossed to Ulrich's Mercedes. He propped his ass on the hood and leaned back to wait. It didn't take long for the receptionist to register what he was doing. He watched through the glass-paneled door as she hustled away to inform her boss that the nasty lawyer hadn't gone away. A few minutes later Ulrich barreled out the front door, his face already flushed with temper.

"Get off my car. If I find so much as a scratch on it, I'll call the police. See how you like being arrested for damaging private property."

Quinn didn't budge.

"Last time I looked there wasn't a law against sitting on a car. But go right ahead. I'm very interested to hear your views on respecting private property, and I'm sure the police are, too."

Ulrich pulled his phone out but didn't attempt to dial. "If you've come here to negotiate on that girl's behalf, you need to talk to my lawyer."

Quinn ran his eyes over Ulrich's silk suit and shiny loafers. The guy clearly fancied himself a player. Amazing how a little bit of success could go to a person's head.

Quinn stood, sliding his fingertips into his front pockets. "You and I both know what you've been trying to do to Amy Parker. It's going to stop. And this stupid defamation suit is going to disappear. You got that?"

For a moment Ulrich looked shocked at Quinn's directness. Then he smiled and rocked back on his heels. "You don't scare me. I can hire guys like you by the truckload. The smartest thing you can do is convince your girlfriend to back out of the deal she made with council. Tell her if she does it within the next week, I'll even think about letting her have her deposit back."

"If that's the way you want to play it. Just so you know, I'll be representing Amy for free in all her dealings with you. I can stall and block and delay, file motions back and forth for years. Guys like me live for that shit. And it won't cost Amy a cent. I hope you've got a big budget for legal expenses, Barry."

"We'll see." Ulrich's confident smile was still in place. *Smug prick.*

Quinn had a childish urge to shove him backward, maybe swing a punch or two. But there were better ways to hurt a small man desperate to better himself in the world.

"I've been doing a bit of reading up on you," he said. "You're a lucky guy. Lots of growth over the past five years, lots of big, fat contracts coming your way."

"If you've got a point, make it. I've got things to do."

Quinn's hand flexed. *Just one punch...*

"Here's my point. You make life uncomfortable for Amy and I'll make things uncomfortable for you. A few

phone calls to the right people and I can get the Australian Securities and Investment Commission to review
your annual returns. I can make enough noise about the
blatant favoritism inherent in your fast-tracked planning
approvals to merit a full inquiry into your relationship
with council by the state government. I can suggest the
tax department take a look at your records for the past
five years. I can hound you to hell and back again."

Ulrich's smile remained in place but a muscle flickered at the corner of his eye.

"Is your company up to that kind of scrutiny, Barry?
Are all your business dealings squeaky-clean and above
reproach?" Quinn pulled his keys from his pocket.
"Because if they're not, if you've slipped up even once,
I'm going to nail you to the wall."

Quinn clapped the other man on the shoulder a little
too firmly and headed for his car. He could feel Ulrich
glaring at him every step of the way. Good. He'd much
rather Ulrich focus his enmity on him instead of Amy.

Quinn slid behind the wheel and started the engine.
Ulrich was on his phone, his back turned. Calling his
lawyer, no doubt.

Quinn shrugged. Ulrich was a bully, an impatient one.
He was used to people rolling over for him but Quinn
doubted he had the stomach for a long, drawn-out fight.

At least he hoped not. But if the other man did dig in,
Quinn would make him hurt in as many ways possible.

Whatever it took to protect Amy.

THE FOLLOWING AFTERNOON, Amy put down the electric
sander and shook out her hands. She was covered from
head to toe in a fine film of white powder from sanding
the walls in the balcony. She pulled the disposable dust

mask off her face and ran her hand over her hair. A cloud of powder puffed around her.

Now that the sander was quiet, she could hear Quinn working downstairs. The squeak of the scaffolding as he shifted his weight. The low sound of his voice singing along with Nickelback.

She moved the ladder across a few feet but paused before climbing it and starting on the next section of wall.

She and Quinn had hardly talked all day. She'd thought that her many, many years of experience in hiding her feelings would mean she was a natural at pretending it was business as usual between them, but she could barely meet his eyes when he arrived for work this morning. He'd seemed equally uncomfortable, and things had deteriorated from there.

So much for both of them being cool with what had happened.

She heard the sound of a cell phone ringing in the theatre, then the low tones of Quinn's voice. She deliberately tuned out. His private life was none of her business.

Still, she noticed when he ended the call, and she tensed when she heard his footsteps on the stairs. He was coming up to talk to her.

Even though she knew she probably looked as though she'd been rolled in flour thanks to all the plaster dust, she pushed her hair back from her face and adopted a casual expression that was supposed to convey how unaffected she was by Quinn and the world in general. She even picked up the sander to make it look as though she hadn't been standing around mooning over him for the last five minutes.

"Hey," he said as he appeared in the archway to the upper foyer.

She took an involuntary step backward. Sometime between lunchtime and now he'd taken his sweatshirt off. She stared at the snug navy tank top he was wearing underneath, taking in his big shoulders and well-muscled arms and flat belly.

"Hey," she said, a shade too late.

It wasn't fair. He worked at a desk. He had no business having a chest and arms and shoulders like that. If she'd known she was lying on top of all that gorgeous muscle yesterday, she would have torn his clothes off with her teeth.

"How's it going up here?" He cast an eye over the walls.

"Okay," she said. She started fiddling with the sander. Even though she'd just put a new sheet of sandpaper in, changing it would give her an excellent excuse for not looking at Quinn any more than she had to.

She braced the unit between her knees while she worked on the clamps to release the paper.

"What's up?" she asked.

"I ran into Rick Bachelor in the street again earlier."

"Oh, yeah?" She fumbled the clamp and swore softly. She saw Quinn take a step toward her out of the corner of her eye.

"You want a hand?"

"I'm fine," she said a little too sharply. No way was she going to be able to retain the pretense that she was indifferent to him if he invaded her personal space.

She kept her attention on the sander but she was pretty sure her cheeks were turning pink. There was a small silence before Quinn spoke again.

"I asked Rick if he and Naomi wanted to come over for dinner and he just called to confirm. So I was thinking maybe you could—"

"No." The word was out of her mouth before she'd even consciously thought it. She knew what he was about to ask. Rick and Naomi were both old school friends and Amy liked them a lot but no way was she sitting beside Quinn at a dinner party as though the two of them were a matched set. It was way too close to what her heart wanted.

"You don't even know what I was going to ask yet," Quinn said.

She jerked the sandpaper free from the clamps. "You were going to ask me over for dinner, right?"

"Yeah."

"I'm busy. I'm having dinner with Denise." It wasn't a complete lie. She did owe Denise dinner and tonight was as good a time as any.

"She could come, as well. I was thinking of doing a roast. My one foolproof meal."

He smiled self-deprecatingly. She was already shaking her head.

"Thanks, but I think she wanted to talk about some girl stuff. Problems with her latest boyfriend. You know."

She snuck a look at Quinn from beneath her eyelashes. He was watching her intently, his expression unreadable.

"Maybe another night," she forced herself to say.

"Yeah."

She straightened. "Better get back to it."

She turned her back on him.

Go away. Take your bloody impressive chest and too-tight tank top and go back downstairs and leave me be.

"Ames."

He didn't say anything else and she knew he was waiting for her to face him. She didn't want to. She felt stretched thin from all the pretending she'd had to do today.

She steeled herself and relented.

"Are we okay?" he asked.

"Yeah. Of course we are. Why wouldn't we be?"

He simply stared at her. Okay, that had been a stupid thing to say. A little too casual, given the circumstances.

"I'm fine. Just a bit tired, that's all," she amended.

"Me, too. Didn't sleep much last night."

The memory of yesterday's encounter hung in the air between them like a tangible thing. Any second now he was going to bring it up again, tell her again how much he valued her friendship and how dumb it had been.

"I really need to do this," she said, gesturing with the sander. "I want to try to get this wall finished by tonight."

This time Quinn didn't say anything when she turned away from him. She waited until she heard him descending the stairs before she pulled out her cell phone and called Denise.

SHE HAD A HEADACHE by the time she arrived at the Lake House restaurant that night. She sat in the car for a moment before heading inside.

I don't know if I can keep doing this.

But it wasn't as though she had a choice. She'd tried cutting Quinn out of her life and it hadn't worked. She'd made her move and he'd told her it was a mistake. She was all out of options.

She slid out of the car.

Denise was waiting at their table, sipping on a cocktail. She'd curled her hair and was wearing a low-cut red dress that barely contained her generous breasts.

"Wow. You look like a Playboy bunny," Amy said admiringly.

"Thanks. I figured I might as well pull out all the stops. Never know when a lonely millionaire might be having dinner on his own."

Denise cast a hopeful glance around the restaurant. The only man dining alone had silver hair and a walking cane. They both watched as he cut his steak into small, manageable portions.

"It's a nice theory," Amy said diplomatically.

"Pity it sucks in practice."

They both laughed and picked up their menus.

"Let's get some wine. I need alcohol more than I need air right now," Amy said.

They ordered champagne, then a bottle of sauvignon blanc with their meal. As usual, Denise was good company, full of shamelessly exaggerated stories about her recent dating experiences and anecdotes from her large, boisterous family. By the time they were nibbling on dessert Amy had one elbow on the table and was having trouble forming her vowel sounds. Which was perfect—exactly where she wanted to be. Pleasantly anesthetized. Numb.

She was just thinking about how nice it was to relax and forget about the tensions of the week when Denise brought the conversation round to Quinn.

"Must be pretty good having Quinn back in town. You guys were always so close."

Instantly Amy's shoulders got tight. "Yeah. So close. No one closer than us." She poked at her sticky date pudding with a fork.

"It's a shame about the divorce. But you've got to ask yourself, how many teen romances survive all the crappola life throws at you? Not many, in my opinion."

"I guess."

"So how long do you think it'll be before he's married again?"

Amy nearly spilled her wine. "What is it with everyone trying to marry Quinn off again when he's not even properly divorced yet?"

"I don't know. He seems like the kind of guy who should be married. I bet he'd make a great husband."

There was no way Amy was drunk enough to have this conversation. "You still thinking about taking up ballroom dancing?" she asked a little desperately. "I've always wanted to learn how to tango."

"Do you know if he's seeing anyone? Because I have to say, I wouldn't mind slinging my hook in that direction. At all. If you get my drift."

Dear God.

That was all Amy needed. Yet another of her friends seducing Quinn right in front of her.

"You know what? Let's talk about something else."

For the first time Denise seemed to register her discomfort. "What's wrong?"

"Not a thing in the world. I just don't want to talk about Quinn Whitfield all night."

"It's hardly been all night. I asked a few questions—"

"Well there's no point asking me, because I have no idea what Quinn wants. Never have, never will."

Amy lifted her glass and gulped the last of her wine. When she lowered it again Denise was watching her with narrowed eyes.

"Did you and Quinn have a fight or something?"

"No siree. Quinn and I are best buds. Pals. He values my friendship. Wouldn't ever want to do anything to ruin it."

Denise's jaw dropped and she opened her eyes so wide

Amy was afraid they were going to pop right out of her head.

"Oh. My. God."

"What?"

"You're hot for Quinn."

For a moment Amy froze like a bunny in the car headlights. Then she made a rude noise. "Am not. Don't be ridiculous."

"Bull. Shit. You want to get busy with him. You want to climb him like a cat on a curtain," Denise said with undisguised relish.

"You're wrong. Way wrong. We grew up together. He's like my brother."

Denise slowly shook her head, her red curls bobbing. "Pretty convincing, Ames, but I'm not buying. I always wondered about you two, you know. I mean, he's so hot. Those dark eyes. That ass. Sometimes I get sweaty just looking at him. And you guys have always been so close." A new thought seemed to cross her mind. "My God, how do you stand it?"

Amy stared at her friend. For a second all the denials she should make hovered on the tip of her tongue. She'd held her secret to her chest for years, fully aware that once it was revealed she'd become an object of pity to her friends and family. Poor Amy, chasing a lost dream. But the past few days had been so confusing, so damned hard. The temptation of sharing her innermost thoughts with someone else was too strong to resist.

"I have no idea. At the moment, I'm seriously thinking about going to the doctor and asking him to prescribe something to turn the clock back to prepuberty. Just for the month that Quinn is in town. That, or I'm going to have to borrow that sex catalog you keep talking about and buy something big and scary and industrial."

Denise did the eye-popping thing again. "Wow. I was right. You have got it bad."

Amy leaned across the table and pointed a finger at her friend. "You have no idea how bad. Get this. I've been in love with Quinn since we were both fourteen. How 'bout them apples?"

In for a penny, in for a pound, right?

Denise blinked, then her mouth turned down at the corners. "Oh, Ames, that's so sad."

Amy thumped her fist on the table. "No! Don't you dare feel sorry for me!" She said it so loudly that several heads turned. "I'm fine. I've been fine. I will continue to be fine. Loving someone you can never have is not the end of the world. It's not like I don't have a rich and fulfilling life. Big deal if one tiny aspect of it is not perfect. It's not the end of the world."

"You already said that."

"Because it bears repeating," Amy said, thumping the table one last time, just to ensure she'd made her point.

She looked around for their waiter and gestured him over to the table.

"Could we have another bottle of wine, please?" she asked.

"Maybe another bottle isn't such a great idea. I don't think I've ever seen you this drunk."

"Another bottle is the best idea I've had all week. I feel great."

"Right." Denise wiped the corners of her mouth with her napkin. "So, does Quinn know how you feel?"

Amy rolled her eyes. "No."

"Why not?"

"Because we're *friends*. And as soon as I tell him how I feel everything will be weird and awkward and wrong and nothing will ever be the same again."

"Maybe. But what if he feels the same?"

"He doesn't. Believe me." Amy focused on the waiter as he appeared to fill her glass. "Leave the bottle, thanks."

"How do you know if you've never asked?"

Amy made a big show out of pretending to think it over, cocking her head to one side theatrically. "Hmm. Let me see. Because he married someone else after going out with her exclusively for most of our high school years? That was a bit of a giveaway."

"But he's getting a divorce. He's a single guy now."

Amy took a big slug of wine. "He's not interested in me. He'll never see me as more than his friend."

Denise opened her mouth. Then she closed it without saying anything.

Amy eyed her over the top of her glass. "What?"

"Nothing."

"Come on, 'Nise. You're dying to say something. I can practically see the words forming in a speech bubble above your head." Amy stumbled over the word *practically,* but she was confident Denise got the gist of it.

"Okay, fine. I never thought I'd see the day when Amy Parker was a pussy about something."

Amy blinked. "A pussy. You're calling me a *pussy?*"

"That's right, I am. A big old pussy. Meow."

Amy jabbed a thumb at her own chest. "I threw a muffin at Barry Ulrich's head. That's how much of a pussy I am."

Denise waved a hand in the air, dismissing the muffin assault with the flick of her brightly lacquered nails.

"Everyone wants to throw a muffin at Barry Ulrich's head. You might have been the first but you won't be the last."

"I took on the council," Amy said. "I saved and planned for ten years to buy the Grand. Those are all pretty non-pussy things."

"They are. But being in love with Quinn for sixteen years and not telling him how you feel now that he's available cancels them out big-time."

"It does not." Amy couldn't believe Denise was giving her a hard time over this. She'd expected sympathy and support after spilling her big secret, not a pep talk on being assertive.

"You need to tell him," Denise said.

"You're nuts."

"What's the worst thing that could happen?"

Amy slurped more wine before answering. "He could laugh at me. Worse, he could feel sorry for me."

"He might. But he might not."

"That's not a risk I'm prepared to take."

"So you'll live your whole life never knowing?"

Amy leaned both elbows on the table and prepared to fully humiliate herself.

"If you must know, I laid a kiss on him yesterday and he freaked out. Told me he thought it was a bad idea for us to be anything other than friends. So I think I have a fair idea how he feels. Mystery solved, case closed."

Denise sat straighter in her chair. "You kissed? You and Quinn? Did he kiss you back? How long did it last?"

"Not long enough," Amy said darkly.

"But Quinn kissed you back?"

Amy shrugged dismissively. "It didn't mean anything. He was being kind. Quinn's always kind."

"Guys don't kiss women because they're being *kind,* Ames."

"They do if they've been friends for thirty years."

"Was it just a kiss? Did he go past first base?"

"I'm not going to answer that."

Denise gasped. "He did! How far past? Second base?" *"Denise."*

"Oh my God. He got to third base, didn't he?"

Amy glared at her friend. "None of your business."

"Third base is not kindness. Definitely. Third base is lust. Quinn has the hots for you." Denise said it unequivocally, as though it was fact, beyond contradiction or argument.

Amy shook her head. Her brain sloshed around thickly and the room shifted on its axis. Okay, maybe the third bottle of wine had been a bad idea. "He was being polite."

Denise reached across the table and grabbed both of Amy's hands. "Listen to me. I know you're as drunk as a skunk or we wouldn't even be having this conversation, but you need to talk to Quinn. Men do not put their hands down the panties of women they do not want to have sex with. Trust me. I've had enough hands in my panties to know."

Amy squeezed her friend's hand and blinked. Three Denises wobbled in front of her, all of them watching her with fond concern. "You're a sweetie. I appreciate you cheering me on from the sidelines. But I think I need to go to the bathroom now and throw up."

She staggered to her feet and made her way across the dining room to the ladies'. Once she was in a cubicle she braced herself and waited for her dinner to make a return appearance. Nothing happened, and after a few minutes the world stopped spinning quite so madly and her stomach settled.

A rap sounded on the cubicle door.

"Ames. How you doing?" Denise asked.

"I'm okay. No regurgitation to speak of so far."

"Always a good sign. Want me to call you a cab?"

"It's okay. I can do it."

Ten minutes later she was stumbling up the gravel drive to her cottage.

"Drink lots of water" had been Denise's last words before she rolled Amy into the cab, but it was what she'd said over dessert that Amy couldn't get out of her head.

"Am not a pussy," she told her front door. She stabbed the key repeatedly at the lock until it slid into the slot, then shuffled her way into the house.

Just because she'd chosen a lifetime of friendship over the possibility of something happening between her and the man she loved did not make her a coward. It made her sensible. Practical. Realistic.

She toed off her high heels and walked to the kitchen, zigzagging from one wall to the other. She flung open the pantry door and dug around until she found a dusty old bottle of port hidden up the back behind the spices.

"Knew you were in there somewhere," she said to the bottle. She poured herself a good glassful and sipped at it, pulling a face at how sweet it was after the crispness of the Semillon sauvignon she'd been drinking with dinner.

Still, it was the only alcohol she had in the house and it would do the trick.

I never thought I'd see the day when Amy Parker was a pussy about something.

Amy growled and took a big gulp of port. "Get out of my head."

But Denise simply wouldn't bugger off. She followed

Amy into the bathroom, calling her a coward and asking the same thing over and over.

What's the worst thing that could happen?
What's the worst thing that could happen?
What's the worst thing that could happen?

Amy stared at her reflection. The answer came from a place deep inside her.

"I could find out once and for all that he doesn't feel the same way that I do."

She blinked.

Wow.

Denise was right: she really was a pussy.

She was too afraid to find out there really was no hope. She preferred to live in a kind of never-never land where she could angst over Quinn but still indulge the fantasy that one day, maybe, if the moon and planets were all aligned, he might possibly return her feelings.

Amy gripped the edge of the bathroom sink until her knuckles were white. She stared at herself in the mirror for a long, drawn-out moment. Then she nodded.

"Fine. If that's the way it has to be."

Then she swiveled on her heel and went looking for a pair of shoes.

CHAPTER NINE

SHE JAMMED HER FEET into her purple sneakers and made for the door. She remembered to grab her house keys at the last moment, then she was outside in the cold night air. She thought about going back for a jacket, but it seemed like a lot of hassle and she had things to do, people to see. One person in particular.

Her parents' street was three blocks over from her own. There was a sickle moon riding high in the sky. She had to really concentrate to keep walking in a straight line. It came to her gradually that it was possible she was too drunk to be undertaking such an important mission. But she was also aware she probably wouldn't even be considering doing what she was about to do if she was any closer to sobriety.

She turned in to her parents' street and walked past their house to the Whitfield place. The front windows glowed from within, a sure sign that Quinn was still awake.

Good.

She negotiated her way up his driveway safely but tripped on the top step to the porch, barreling into the front door with her arms outstretched. For some reason this struck her as being very funny—so graceful, so elegant, especially when she was about to offer Quinn her heart on a silver platter. She was giggling like a school-girl when the front door swung open.

"Amy. Jesus. I thought it was the world's biggest possum," Quinn said.

"Possums don't wear shoes."

Quinn peered at her. "Have you been drinking?"

"A little. But that's not important. We have bigger fish to fry, friend o' mine."

Quinn raised an eyebrow but stood to one side. "Come on in."

She followed him inside, stopping in her tracks when she got her first good look at him under decent lighting. He was barefoot and wearing a pair of very dark jeans and a white shirt open at the neck. His sleeves were rolled up over his strong forearms. His dark hair was tousled. He had the exact perfect amount of five-o'clock shadow.

He looked good enough to eat. Strong and sexy and gorgeous.

Irresistible.

"Look at you." She threw her hands in the air, exasperated and overwhelmed in equal measure. "I come over here with a little speech all ready to go to kind of ease you into it, and here you are, standing around being so bloody gorgeous and freakin' sexy. How am I supposed to react? What am I supposed to do? Huh? You tell me."

Quinn froze. "What?"

She gestured dramatically again. "God, Quinn, do I have to say it a million times, spell it out for you in ninety-foot letters? What do you want from me? I love you, Quinn Whitfield. I love you, I love you, I love you. There, happy?"

"You're drunk."

She took a step toward him, then another, until they

were standing breast to chest, barely an inch between them. She leaned toward him, just enough to feel the heat of his body against hers. She reached up and grabbed the front of his shirt, her hands curling into fists around the fabric.

"Yes, I am drunk. Very drunk. But that does not change what I am about to say to you. Quinn Whitfield, I have loved you since I was fourteen years old. It absolutely freaking killed me when you got with Lisa that summer, and I cried myself to sleep the night you both got married. I know you're not perfect, but I think you're wonderful. Sexy and clever and strong and talented and sexy. Did I mention that already…?"

She shook her head to clear it. Not a great idea. The room spun a little. Time to cut to the chase.

"Anyway. That's how I feel. I think you're the bee's knees. The cat's pajamas. The ant's pants. If you were mine, there was no way I would ever have even glanced sideways at another man."

She released her grip on his shirt, smoothing the fabric flat against his chest before giving it a little pat and taking a step backward.

"I wasn't going to say anything, but Denise said I was a pussy if I didn't and I am not a pussy. Never have been, never will be. So. Here I am. And that's how I feel."

Quinn was very still. She held her breath, waiting for some sign that her words had struck a chord in him. But he simply looked blank. As though she'd thrown him the biggest curveball of his life.

Then she heard it: a whisper, followed by a muffled laugh. A horrible premonition skittered through her brain. She walked to the living room door and glanced inside.

And saw Rick and Naomi Bachelor sitting on the

couch, coffee cups in front of them, embarrassed smiles on their faces. Sitting opposite them were Jerome Cooper and his wife Lacey. Like Naomi and Rick, Lacey was an old school friend.

"Hey, Amy," Naomi said lamely.

Lacey waved awkwardly. "Long time no see."

"Oh, God," Amy said. She took a step backward.

"Amy," Quinn said. He reached out to grab her elbow.

She jerked away from him, spinning on her heel and lunging toward the front door. "I have to go."

Oh, boy, did she have to go.

Sixteen years she'd waited to declare herself to Quinn Whitfield and she'd done it in front of an audience. Every word she'd said was going to be all over town tomorrow. Everyone would know.

Everyone.

"Amy," Quinn said again, but by some miracle she got the front door open first try. She raced out onto the porch and down the steps to the driveway.

"Amy!"

She broke into a flat-out run. She had no idea where she was going—somewhere quiet and dark to hide for a while. Somewhere she could pretend that she hadn't exposed herself to practically the whole town as well as Quinn.

Somewhere she could close her eyes and pretend she hadn't seen the blank shock on Quinn's face when she'd told him she loved him.

She was convinced she could hear Quinn following her so she tucked her chin into her chest and put on a surge. It was only when she turned the corner, puffing and blowing, that she saw there was no one behind her. Through the alcohol haze she remembered Quinn's house full of dinner guests and the fact that he'd answered the door in bare feet. She was safe. For now.

The moment she stopped running bile burned her throat and she bent over and lost her dinner in front of Mrs. Patterson's roses.

She used the Pattersons' garden tap to rinse her mouth and clean up the mess. Then she headed home, her feet heavier than lead, her shoulders hunched.

The worst thing that could happen had happened: she'd told Quinn she loved him…and he'd said nothing.

Not a thing.

QUINN SWORE UNDER HIS BREATH as he hobbled up the front steps. He'd stepped on something sharp while attempting to chase Amy down. She'd bolted like a jackrabbit, alcohol and distress giving her wings.

He leaned against the porch post and inspected his foot. Sure enough, he had an angry-looking cut across his arch.

"Idiot." He wasn't sure if he was talking to himself or Amy.

He opened the front door and entered the house, pulling up short when he realized his dinner guests were all standing in the front hall shrugging into their coats.

"We'll get out of your hair," Rick said.

"Don't want to overstay our welcome," Lacey added with an awkward smile.

"Nobody is in anybody's hair," he said. Even to his own ears it sounded false.

Naomi reached out and patted his arm. "We figured you'd probably want to go find Amy."

He did. But he also needed a few minutes to process the bombshell Amy had just dropped on him.

Amy loved him?

It didn't seem possible. And yet on some deep, gut-driven, instinctive level it felt right. True. Real.

Lacey and Naomi exchanged looks.

"Listen, Quinn," Lacey said. "Before we go, we wanted to let you know that what happened tonight was none of our business. What we heard won't go further than this room, okay?"

"Yeah, I might be a hairdresser but I know when to keep my lips zipped," Naomi added.

"Thanks. I appreciate it," Quinn said. The last thing he wanted was for Amy to feel stupid or foolish or exposed.

He walked them to their cars and accepted their thanks for the meal, remembering at the last minute that he'd promised Rick over dinner that he'd take a look at a property contract the other man was worried about.

"Drop it by the Grand tomorrow if you like," Quinn said.

Rick's face lit up. "Really? I know it's small fry compared to the stuff you normally do up in Sydney, but I'd really appreciate a second opinion."

"No worries. Drop it by," Quinn assured him.

He watched them drive off, then he returned to the house and closed the door behind him. For a long moment he simply stood in the empty silence of his childhood home, his mind resonating with one thought: Amy loved him.

He remembered the heartfelt sincerity in her big brown eyes as she'd grabbed his shirt and made her declaration. Yes, she'd been rip-roaring drunk, but she'd meant every word she'd said.

He limped to the bathroom and wiped the dirt out of the cut on his foot. Then he pulled on socks and his boots and grabbed his car keys.

Four minutes later he pulled up in front of Amy's house. The windows were dark but he climbed the steps and knocked on her front door anyway. She didn't answer and he knocked again. He knew she was home—could feel her presence in the house. He tried the door, but it was locked.

"Amy. Let me in," he called.

Nothing.

"Amy. Come on. We need to talk."

He tried for another ten minutes, then he called her landline and her cell. She didn't pick up. Finally he got in his car and drove home.

He walked into his parents' living room and stared at the coffee cups and dessert plates left over from dinner.

He didn't know what to do. That was the truth of it. Amy's words were echoing inside him, over and over. And he didn't know what to do.

I have loved you since I was fourteen years old.

It absolutely freaking killed me when you got with Lisa that summer.

I cried myself to sleep the night you both got married.

He rubbed his jaw.

He hated the thought of Amy being in pain because of something he'd done. Or not done. Couldn't stand it.

He thought back to the day of his wedding, remembered Amy standing with them at the altar as both bridesmaid and best man—"best person," as she'd insisted on being called. She'd smiled and laughed with them, cheered when they exchanged vows. Been the best friend that both he and Lisa had expected of her.

Then she'd gone home that night and cried herself to sleep. Because of him. Over him.

"Shit. *Shit.*"

He had no idea how to sort out his feelings. Guilt and fear and regret and sadness, all mixed up together.

He hadn't known. Had never even had a clue. If he had, he would have—

What would he have done?

He sat on the edge of the couch and put his head in his hands.

What would he have done? What would have happened if Amy had declared herself years ago during that long, hot summer when they'd all been fourteen and he'd been thinking about her and dreaming about her? What if it had been Amy who'd leaned across his French textbook and looked him in the eyes and told him she thought he was hot and she wanted to kiss him, the way Lisa had?

He closed his eyes as a cascade of possibilities flashed across his mind, a whole alternative life.

After a moment he opened his eyes again.

The truth was, he would never know. Because it was Lisa he'd hooked up with that summer, and it was Lisa he'd fallen in love with and it was Lisa he'd married.

And it was Lisa who'd betrayed him, and Lisa he was about to divorce.

He couldn't go back. And, in all honesty, he wouldn't want to. Even though things had not turned out great with Lisa, the two of them had had their moments. He'd been happy, definitely, for some of their time together. He had loved her.

But their marriage was over now and he was free to find a new way forward. A new future.

And Amy loved him.

Amy, whose firm, warm little body had been obsessing him all week. Amy, whom he'd loved wholeheartedly as his great friend since before he even understood what the word meant. Amy, who could always make him laugh, who could infuriate and challenge him like no other, who had shared so much with him.

He scrubbed his face with his hands, suddenly understanding the full import of Amy's visit this evening. She'd declared herself to him. After sixteen years. And she'd be expecting an answer. A response.

She'd want to know how he felt. What he wanted. If their friendship was to remain a friendship or become something else.

The thought brought him to his feet again. He moved to the fireplace to poke at the dying embers of the fire. Then he crossed to the window to stare out at the darkened street.

He loved Amy. That was a given. He desired her. But Amy didn't just want sex from him. She wanted a relationship, a future. Not exactly your typical dating situation. In fact, it took the concept of performance anxiety to a whole new level. Every word, every action, every emotion would be loaded with sixteen years of expectation, anticipation and history.

In a few weeks' time he was going to be a divorced man. A very different man from the twenty-four-year-old baby lawyer who'd exchanged vows with his teen love six years ago. His marriage and breakup and divorce had left the inevitable marks on him. He wouldn't be human if they hadn't. He was angry and a bit bitter. Hurt. He suspected it might be hard for him to trust again, to take someone at their word.

He was also partner in a profitable, lucrative commercial law firm in Sydney, hundreds of miles away from the old cinema Amy had thrown her heart and soul into. He had responsibilities. Obligations.

There were so many things that could go wrong. So many things that might not match up. That was what it all came down to in the end: the potential for disaster. More than anything, he didn't want to disappoint or hurt Amy.

He went to bed and stared at the ceiling. No stunning insights came to him in the wee hours. When morning came, he had absolutely no idea what he was going to say to her.

He forced himself to make a few decisions before rolling out of bed. He would tell Amy that he was attracted to her. Very much so.

He would tell her that he loved spending time with her.

And he would tell her about his doubts. And his fears. And he would see what she said in return.

He drove to the Grand with a belly full of knots. This was Amy, after all. He was desperate not to screw things up between them.

As he'd half suspected, she wasn't waiting for him. She'd been so plastered last night that the odds were excellent she'd woken with a hangover. He bought himself a take-out coffee and settled in to wait.

Her car turned in to the lot forty minutes later. His chest tightened the moment he saw her. She parked next to him and he smiled faintly when he saw she was wearing a baseball cap and big sunglasses. Definitely hungover, then.

She grabbed her handbag from the passenger seat then slid out of the car at the same time that he got out of his.

"Hey," she said across the roof.

"Hey."

"Sorry to keep you waiting."

"No worries. Figured you might be a little late this morning. After last night."

He'd meant the comment as a way in to the conversation they needed to have, but Amy surprised him by groaning and clapping a hand to her forehead.

"Oh, God. Don't tell me I came to your place last night, as well?"

He took a moment to respond. "You could say that."

"It's official. You can't take me anywhere. How embarrassing." She pushed her sunglasses a little higher on her nose. "According to Denise, I drank nearly three bottles of wine on my own last night. Can you believe that? She poured me into a taxi and sent me home. Then apparently I rolled up at her place a few hours later, wanting to party like it was 1999. I suppose you're going to tell me I did the same thing to you, huh?"

Quinn had been drunk with Amy plenty of times over the years. He'd listened to her ramble on and on for hours about Art Deco architecture and the golden years of cinema, held her hair away from her face while she vomited, fed her coffee and egg-and-bacon sandwiches to cure her hangovers the next day. Not once had he ever known her to black out.

He had to admit, it was a novel way of dealing with the situation: pretend it had never happened. Or, at the very least, that she didn't remember that it had happened. The emotional equivalent of an ostrich sticking its head in the sand.

"You mostly wanted to talk, not party," he said slowly.

She groaned again. "I really embarrassed myself, didn't I? What did I do? Please tell me I didn't yack on your mother's Persian rug."

Some of the tension eased from Quinn's shoulders. No matter what concerns he had about the future of their relationship, he couldn't help but be amused by the zeal with which she was throwing herself into her attempt at damage control.

Meryl Streep, eat your heart out.

"You didn't yack on the rug," he said, unable to suppress a smile.

"Bless you. One piece of good news this morning. I feel like someone parked a cement truck on my head overnight."

She pressed her fingers to her forehead dramatically and started to recount some of the crazy antics she'd gotten up to at Denise's place.

He watched her, admiring the performance. The throw-away breeziness, the self-deprecating jokes. He could guess exactly what had happened—she'd woken with cotton mouth and a hammering headache and remembered what she'd done. Knowing Amy, she'd probably squirmed with self-recrimination and embarrassment for a while. Then she'd come up with a plan to minimize how vulnerable she was no doubt feeling right now.

Not a very good plan, admittedly, but a plan nonetheless. And she'd been desperate enough to put that not-very-good plan into action.

A huge wave of tenderness and affection washed over him as he stood in the early morning sunshine listening to his best friend pile on the baloney.

She was an idiot. An adorable, gorgeous, feisty, funny, sweet, sexy idiot.

He waited until she paused to draw breath.

"Ames. Come on. This is me."

She started to say something, then shut her jaw with a click. He could practically hear her debating with herself, trying to decide if she should give her too-drunk-to-be-responsible-for-my-own-actions gambit another shot or not. Then her shoulders slumped and she reached up to tug her cap lower on her face.

"Could we please not talk about this?" she asked, her voice anguished.

"I think we should."

"Well, I don't. Let's forget it ever happened."

"Sorry, Ames, but it's not something I'm going to forget in a hurry."

"You should. You should just wipe it from your mind. That's what I'm going to do."

"Ames." He reached for her sunglasses, sick of not being able to see her eyes.

She shied away from him. "Don't! Don't be kind to me, Quinn. Just…don't."

Kind? What the hell was she talking about?

"Listen—"

He broke off as a black Audi convertible drove out of the alley and turned in to the parking lot.

Amy made a surprised sound as it drew to a halt.

"Isn't that…?"

He eyed the car's dark tinted windows. "Yeah."

He watched as his soon-to-be ex-wife slid out of the car, a vision in stylish black. Their eyes met across twenty feet of gravel.

"Quinn," she said.

"Lisa."

What the hell was she doing here?

"Amy. It is you under that hat and glasses, right?" Lisa said as she crossed the distance between them. "You look like you're hiding from the paparazzi."

"It's me," Amy said. Her voice cracked on the last word. She cleared her throat.

Lisa leaned forward and kissed her. "It's really good to see you," she said quietly. She stepped back and shifted her focus to Quinn. "Don't worry, I'm not about to kiss you."

She said it lightly, wryly, but he frowned.

"I thought we were doing this through our lawyers," he said.

She seemed a little taken aback by his directness, but he didn't see the point in beating around the bush.

"We are. I'm not here to see you. I'm here to see Amy."

"Sorry?" Amy sounded startled.

"I came to see you," Lisa repeated.

Quinn crossed his arms over his chest. He might not live with her any more, but he still knew when Lisa was lying.

"Is it too early for brunch?" Lisa asked. She very carefully kept her gaze on Amy, avoiding eye contact with him.

Amy slid a look toward Quinn. She looked torn, uncomfortable.

"Um, sure. I mean, no. It's not too early," she said.

Lisa smiled brightly and shook her head so that her long, straight hair flipped down her back. "Let's go somewhere nice. My treat. I saw a new place on the way in. Sault or something like that?"

"Yeah. It's got a good reputation," Amy said. She slid another look Quinn's way.

"We can take my car," Lisa said. She moved toward the Audi.

Amy hesitated before following her, glancing at him. "Um. I'll see you later, okay?"

He nodded. She didn't move. He didn't need to see her eyes to know she was feeling guilty.

"It's okay," he said. "Give me the keys and I'll finish off that last wall in the main theatre."

"You don't have to keep working when I'm slacking off."

He held out his hand. "Give me the keys."

He thought she was going to argue but after a beat she reached into her pocket and held out her key ring.

"Don't work too hard, okay?"

He wrapped his hands around the keys and her hand. "This conversation isn't over. You know that, right?"

She pulled her hand free. "That's a matter of opinion."

"No, it isn't."

She glanced over her shoulder to where Lisa was watching them. "I have to go."

He let her go. For the time being.

AMY WAS QUIET during the drive to the restaurant. Lisa's unexpected arrival was like a slap in the face. A brutal, very effective, cosmic wake-up call.

For all the days that Quinn had been in town, Amy had only ever thought about him and her, about their friendship and the risk her feelings posed to it. She hadn't once thought about Lisa, about how her friend would feel if, by some miracle, something happened between Amy and Quinn. But the truth was that there had always been three people in this love triangle. And somehow, over the past few days, Amy had allowed herself to forget that.

And no, Lisa's betrayal of Quinn did not cancel out any obligation Amy had toward her friend. Two wrongs didn't make a right.

"I'd forgotten how beautiful it is around here in autumn," Lisa said as they turned onto the road to the restaurant.

Amy studied the towering oaks that lined the road, each a study in ochre, crimson and amber, their leaves lit up like fire by the morning sun.

"I forget to look sometimes," she said. "I guess it's true what they say, familiarity does breed contempt."

"Story of my life."

Lisa said it so quietly Amy almost didn't hear her. Amy flicked her a glance as they pulled in to the parking lot at the restaurant.

"Good, it looks as though they're open," Lisa said.

They were shown to a seat on the rear verandah with a view over lush, colorful garden beds and down a grassy slope toward a dam. Everything was perfect, from the pristine tablecloth to the expensive exotic flowers spilling from a nearby urn. It wasn't until the waiter was flicking a crisp linen napkin over her lap that Amy was able to see past her guilt to register how underdressed she was. Her ragged jeans and green-and-blue striped sweater had seen many better days. Her sneakers were scuffed and she wasn't wearing a shred of makeup. By contrast, Lisa looked as sleek and polished as if she'd just left a photo shoot.

Nothing new there. Ever since the summer of the red bikini, Amy had been standing in Lisa's fashionable, sexy shadow. Why should anything have changed simply because they hadn't seen each other for a while?

"Mmm. The bruschetta looks good. And there's French toast made with brioche. Yum," Lisa said, after studying the menu.

Amy's stomach churned uneasily at the thought of food, particularly food that came accompanied with maple syrup. "I think I'll have black coffee with a side of black coffee."

Lisa gave her a sympathetic look. "I thought you were looking a little under the weather. Big night, huh?"

"You could say that."

"Have the omelet. The protein will do you good," Lisa advised.

She took charge of the ordering when their waiter came, then they both sat back in their seats and regarded each other.

"You look good, Ames," Lisa said. "It's hard to tell under the hat, but your hair's much shorter, yeah?"

"Mmm. More by accident than intention," Amy admitted. "I got chewing gum caught in it a couple of months ago and had to lose four inches."

Lisa laughed, but her smile quickly faded and she shifted nervously in her chair. "I know you're probably wondering why I'm here. Why I wanted to talk to you."

For an absurd, irrational moment Amy thought that Lisa knew. That somehow she'd gotten wind of the kiss and Amy's confession and that she'd come to confront her with her perfidy.

Then sanity returned and she released her grip on the arms of her chair and tried to calm her pounding heart.

"To be honest, I'm still kind of getting over the surprise of seeing you so suddenly."

"It's like this, Ames—I'm seeing a therapist." Lisa blurted it like a kid swallowing cod liver oil, as though she was trying to get the awfulness over and done with as quickly as possible.

Of all the things Amy had expected her friend to say, this was the last. Lisa had never been big on self-exploration and contemplation.

She was aware that Lisa was watching her tensely, waiting for her reaction. She tried to formulate a reply.

"Are you finding it helpful?"

"You think I'm nuts, don't you?" Lisa asked.

"No! Of course not. God, it's not like I couldn't benefit from professional intervention half the time."

Like last night, for example.

"You're the first person I've told. In case you couldn't tell." Lisa smiled self-deprecatingly.

It was Amy's turn to squirm in her chair. There was no way Lisa would be confiding in her if she knew what Amy had done, what Amy wanted. No way.

"So what made you…you know?" Amy asked.

"Seek professional help? Get my head read? It all caught up with me, Ames. The affair, losing Quinn. My own shitty behavior, in a nutshell." Lisa took a mouthful of water and ice cubes clanked against her tall glass. She met Amy's eyes and shrugged. "I told myself I was fine, that Stuart and a new life was what I wanted. I even started looking at houses, was on the verge of putting an offer in on this amazing place in Vaucluse…. Then suddenly I couldn't get out of bed in the morning, and I couldn't stop crying. Stuart took me to the doctor's and he wanted to put me on antidepressants. But I knew it wasn't a chemical thing. It was a me thing. I'm so screwed up, Ames."

Lisa blinked rapidly. Amy reached across the table and took her friend's hand.

"Just because you screwed up doesn't mean you're screwed up," she said.

"Tell that to my therapist," Lisa joked. "My relationship with my parents…my relationship with Quinn…the way I see myself. Basically, I'm a therapist's wet dream. Paula's going to be able to name a ski lodge after me by the time she's straightened me out."

Amy could hear the pain beneath Lisa's lighthearted words.

"I think you're very brave," Amy said. And she meant it. It took a lot of guts to confront your own bad decisions and try to learn from them. "Lots of other people would have taken the tablets and bought the house and never looked back."

"Well, if I could have got away with it I would have," Lisa said. "But apparently my subconscious had other ideas."

"You're still brave."

"We'll see. Anyway, my therapist is the reason why I'm here. We've been talking a lot lately about when I was growing up. You and me and Quinn. God, we used to have fun, didn't we? Remember the time we had that party when my parents were away?"

Amy smiled. "Denise passed out in the backyard and we tried to lock Quinn in the toilet off the laundry room by tying a bit of rope between the door handle and the washing machine."

"But instead of staying trapped, he pulled the washing machine over he yanked on the door so hard," Lisa said.

For some reason they both found this hysterically funny and for a long moment there was nothing but the sound of giggling and wheezing at their table. Lisa fixed Amy with a steady regard once she'd regained her composure.

"I know I messed up with Quinn, and I know how close you two are and how much you'd probably love to punch me in the face for hurting him, but I really don't want to lose you, too, Ames. That's why I'm here. To tell you that I value your friendship. And that if you want to punch me in the face, that's okay with me—as long as we can still be friends."

Guilt wrapped itself around Amy's chest and squeezed hard. If Lisa knew how bad a friend she really was…

"It's not my place to judge you, Lis. At the end of the day, whatever happened is between you and Quinn," she said uncomfortably, "it's none of my business."

"Do you mean that? Really?"

"I wouldn't say it if I didn't."

Lisa sagged with relief. "My God. You have no idea how terrified I was of having this conversation with you. I've been talking about coming down here for weeks, and my therapist has been telling me to do it. But it wasn't until I was lying awake staring at the ceiling last night that I got the courage up. I jumped straight in the car before I could chicken out."

Amy glanced down at her faded sweater and grungy jeans. She didn't consider herself to be a particularly intimidating person. The idea that Lisa had been losing sleep over talking to her was hard to get her head around. "Am I that scary?"

"Hell, yes."

Amy blinked. "Okay." She wasn't sure, but she thought that maybe she was a little offended.

"Not in the way you're thinking," Lisa said quickly. "It's just that you've always been so straight down the line, Ames. You're probably the most honest person I know. Well, you and Quinn, I guess. But then you two were always a matched set. I used to be so jealous of you."

Amy made a scoffing noise. "You're the one with the law degree with honors and the big fancy job and the legs that go on forever and the kind of car I will never, ever be able to afford."

Lisa dismissed it all with the flick of her hand. "You have something that's worth more than any of that, Ames. You know who you are. I've always admired that about you. Why do you think I was always over at your house when we were kids? When I was around you, I felt grounded. You don't bullshit and you care and you're not embarrassed to show it. And you know what counts in life."

Amy felt like a huge fraud. If she was even close to being the person Lisa thought her to be, she'd tell her friend the truth right now. Confess everything, lay it all before her.

Amy looked down and smoothed her fingers along the crease in her napkin. She couldn't do it. Unlike Lisa, she wasn't brave enough to expose her greatest failings to public scrutiny. So much for being a bastion of no-bullshit and honesty.

"I'm no angel, believe me," she said quietly. "I've got my own fair share of flaws, Lisa. More than my share."

The waiter appeared with their meals then and Amy said yes to cracked pepper and no to more sparkling water and made all the right noises about how good her omelet looked.

Lisa leaned forward as the waiter once again left them alone.

"I promise no more heavy talk from now on, Ames. Tell me about your plans for the Grand. And how are your folks? And who should I be on the lookout for while I'm in town?"

Amy forced a smile and took a moment to gather her thoughts. Then she started answering her friend's questions.

CHAPTER TEN

QUINN FINISHED PREPPING the walls in the main theatre. He stopped for a brief chat with Rick when the other man dropped off his contract, then threw himself back into work. By midday the walls were done and he briefly considered going home. Instead he shifted his attention to the concession stand in the foyer. Amy hadn't discussed where she wanted to focus their efforts next but he wasn't in the mood to welcome leisure time.

There was no point lying to himself; it had been a shock seeing Lisa's car turn into the parking lot. Especially given the conversation he'd been having with Amy.

He had no idea why Lisa had chosen to come to town while he was here, but he knew it wasn't a coincidence. He thought about what Duffy had said in his e-mail about having trouble pinning down her lawyer, and used more force than was strictly necessary to push the sander across the pocked and scarred counter. If she was angling for something more in the divorce…

The sander bucked in his hands and he hit the trigger to turn the motor off. He'd hit an exposed nailhead, something he could have avoided if he'd been paying closer attention. He checked, and sure enough, the sandpaper had torn, as well as a corner of the base pad.

Great.

"You look like a ghost."

Quinn glanced over his shoulder. Lisa stood in the front entrance, the afternoon sun turning her hair into a halo and casting her face in shadow. She walked toward him, a tentative smile on her face, her high heels clicking on the marble floor.

"Where's Amy?" he asked, glancing over her shoulder.

"I dropped her at home. She's still pretty hungover. I think she was going to try to have a nap."

He turned back to the concession stand, wiping sawdust off the countertop with his flattened hand. The silence stretched between them but he wasn't about to break it. She was the one who'd come here and sought him out. She could do the heavy lifting.

"Do you really hate me that much, Quinn?"

"I don't hate you."

"You can barely stand to look at me."

She'd always loved a bit of melodrama.

"I'm busy, in case you hadn't noticed. The more stuff I get done while I'm in town, the less Amy has to do on her own."

"You're angry with me."

He turned to face her fully. Clearly, she was determined to have a confrontation.

"What do you expect? You knew I was here, helping Amy. And you suddenly turn up, acting as though it's a coincidence."

"I'm not playing games, Quinn. I've been thinking about home a lot lately. About us, and Amy, how things were when we were all growing up. Do you know that apart from the two times when we broke up in high school and that one time at university, I haven't been single since I was fifteen?"

It was on the tip of his tongue to point out that she'd been so far from single at one time that she'd actually had both a husband *and* a lover, but it would only prolong the discussion.

Six months ago, he would have relished the opportunity to go at her hammer and tongs, lash her with all her wrongs, parade his hurt and sense of betrayal in front of her. Now he didn't see the point. Why waste the energy? They'd been married. He'd given it his best shot. He'd made mistakes. So had she, the last one being a real doozy. What had once been between them was broken, never to be repaired. There was nothing left to do bar sign the papers that dissolved their marriage so they could both move on.

"I don't know what you want from me," he said.

"Well, that makes two of us."

That surprised him. Lisa fiddled with one of her rings. It took him a moment to recognize it as her wedding band, worn on her right hand now.

"Believe it or not, I never meant to hurt you, Quinn. I know that probably sounds disingenuous considering what I did, but it's true. I was so miserable, and I didn't know how to fix anything, so I made it worse."

Man, he hated hearing that she'd been miserable in their marriage, even though he knew it must have been true for her to have the affair. He'd thought over those last years again and again, trying to work out in his own mind what he'd said or not said, done or not done that had pushed her into turning away from him instead of toward him. He'd never come up with a satisfactory answer.

"You want to conduct a postmortem? Is that it?" he asked.

"Do you think it would make any difference?"

"To what?"

"To us. To you being able to look me in the eye and have a civil conversation with me. Maybe even be friends again."

He crossed his arms over his chest. "You want to be friends now?"

Was that what this was all about?

"It would be nice to think that we could salvage something from this mess. We used to be good friends, you and I. We used to enjoy each other. Remember?"

He studied her for a long beat, looking into her clear blue eyes, noting the slight flush on her high cheekbones, the expensive sheen of her hair. She looked beautiful, as always—and very unhappy. He could see it in the way she clenched her hands together, in the tension in the tendons of her neck and the new lines around her eyes. She felt guilty about what had happened, obviously. Wanted to try to make things right between them, ease her conscience.

He shook his head. "We can't turn back the clock, Lis."

"I'm not expecting you to invite me over to your place to hang out and watch the TV or anything. It's just…I miss you. I miss talking with you."

Her quiet words affected him more than he wanted them to. He picked up the sander and started removing the torn sandpaper. As he'd just said, they couldn't turn back the clock.

When he didn't say anything, Lisa cleared her throat. "I guess I'll get out of your hair, then."

She waited a moment longer, giving him one last opportunity to step in. With what, he wondered. Absolution? A knock-knock joke? Then she turned and headed for the door.

He fingered the torn sandpaper once she was gone. She wanted to be friends. She missed him.

He threw the sandpaper in the trash. It pissed him off no end, but he felt guilty for not responding to her overture. Despite all the great reasons he had for not wanting to have her in his life. Which showed how impossible it was to completely sever the emotional ties that had bound the two of them together for so many years.

Perhaps it would be different if they hadn't grown up together as well as having been married. She was part of his personal history in so many ways. She'd been his first kiss, his first girlfriend. She'd been there when he took his first tentative steps into adulthood.

She was right. They had once been good friends. She had a sharp mind and he'd always enjoyed debating the merits of an argument with her. And no one could party like Lisa—when she let her hair down, anything could happen. Some of the worst hangovers of his life could be laid directly at her door. She'd always been generous with praise and gifts and her open-handedness was one of the things he'd loved about her the most.

He'd lost a good friend as well as his wife and lover when she'd betrayed him. And no matter what happened between them in the future, they would never be able to recapture the old ease. It was gone, for good. And it was bloody sad.

Outside, a car sounded its horn and he realized he'd been staring at the silent sander for too long. He checked his watch, then made a decision. Lisa had said she'd dropped Amy at home. It was time for them to finish the conversation they'd started this morning.

He locked up the theatre and headed for his car. In a perfect world, he should probably wait until Amy had had a chance to recover from her hangover with a few hours' sleep before descending on her, but he'd waited all night and most of the day. He wasn't waiting any longer.

His gut was churning by the time he pulled into Amy's street. As much as he hated to admit it, Lisa's visit had thrown him. He parked in front of her house and took a moment to shake the sawdust from his hair, trying to clear his head at the same time. Then he swung the door open and started to climb out of the car.

Do you really hate me that much?

We used to be friends.

We used to enjoy each other.

He froze, one booted foot on the road, the other still in the car as Lisa's words echoed inside him.

If he and Amy entered into a relationship and it failed, would he be having the exact same conversation with her in a few years? Facing the same sense of failure and loss? Would he one day be looking at her with anger in his gut and thinking about how much they'd lost?

He lowered his head and stared at the asphalt.

He thought about Amy, and her drunken declaration, and that kiss…God, that kiss. He thought about Lisa and his divorce and the loss of something that had once been good.

I can't do this.

The thought came from his gut, pure instinct.

No way could he risk losing Amy the way he'd already lost Lisa. Not Amy. She meant too much to him. She was so much a part of him, of his life. If things screwed up… If he let her down or she let him down or if life somehow conspired to throw more at them than they could handle, he didn't know how he would be able to move on from the loss.

He needed her in his life. It was that simple. And if the trade-off for guaranteeing the endurance of their friendship was the sacrifice of his desire to kiss and caress and hold her...then so be it.

He let his breath out on a long, heavy sigh. Then he pulled his foot back into the car, closed the door and started the engine.

As he drove away he thought about how much courage it must have taken for Amy to break sixteen years of silence and declare herself. Some of it had been liquid courage, sure, but he had no doubt that she'd had to work herself up to appearing on his doorstep with her heart in her hands.

He felt as though he was letting her down, denying them a chance without even exploring the potential of what lay between them.

Then he thought about the sadness in Lisa's eyes and the bitter taste his marriage had left in his mouth.

I'm sorry, Ames. I need you in my life too much to risk screwing things up with you, too.

AMY WOKE EARLY the next morning. She showered, ate breakfast and drove to the Grand even though it was barely six.

Once there, she flicked on the lights and did a slow tour, trying to get her head around what needed doing next and not think about the mess that was her private life.

A futile effort, at the best of times.

She stopped by the concession stand, noting that Quinn had made a start on it yesterday. She ran her hand over the newly stripped wood. Then she turned away and climbed the stairs to the upper foyer.

"You're a mad cow," she said to herself as she reached the top. "A mad, irrational, contrary cow."

Because she was angry with Quinn. There was no getting around it. She'd waited all afternoon and all night for him to call or come by her house. Even though she'd told him in no uncertain terms that she wanted to forget all about her declaration. Even though she'd been marinating in guilt since Lisa had unfolded her slim body from her expensive European car and reminded Amy of everything that was at stake.

She'd wanted Quinn to come to her, to force her to discuss what had happened. She'd wanted him to override all her objections and denials and say all the things she'd waited half a lifetime to hear.

Which made her officially crazy, because she already knew how he felt, what he wanted: to be friends. Period. He'd already told her so, after they'd kissed. And he'd told her again with his body language when she'd blurted out her drunken confession. Yet she'd still tensed every time she heard a car in the street last night.

Frustrated with herself, Amy tackled reorganizing their building supplies, forcibly keeping her tangled thoughts at bay with bruising physical labor. By the time she heard Quinn's heavy tread in the rear exit corridor she was covered with sweat from lugging paint cans and ladders around. She stood and wiped her forearm across her forehead as Quinn entered the theatre.

"Hi," she said. Her belly muscles did their usual tighten-release thing at the sight of him, hair still damp from the shower, thighs long and lean in worn denim. She might be angry and disappointed in him, but she still wanted him.

"How did your lunch go?"

"Good. Lis and I had a nice catch-up."

She risked a glance at his face but couldn't get a read on his mood.

"I saw you started on the concession stand," she said. "Should come up well."

"Yeah. Going to take a bit of work, though."

"Yep. Lot of wood there."

"Might need to get some paint stripper onto the carved sections," he said.

"Right. I can get some stuff from the store later. Or you can go grab it if you like…?"

Dear God. This was excruciating. There were so many dead cows in the room it was a wonder either of them could fit.

You did this, Amy. You made things this way.

And the best thing was, there was more to come, thanks to the phone call she'd received from Lisa last night.

"There's something I need to tell you," she said suddenly. Might as well get it over and done with. "Lisa offered to help out at the Grand while she's in town. I didn't know how you'd feel about it. But I didn't want to say no, either. So…"

Quinn's jaw tensed.

"Sorry." It felt woefully inadequate. She was well aware that he hadn't taken time off work so he could rub shoulders with his estranged wife.

"It's not your fault. How long is she here?"

Amy pushed her hair back from her forehead. She hated having a conversation that cast Lisa as the stinky kid, but the reality was that Quinn had every right to not want to spend time with her. It was an awkward situation, any way you looked at it.

"Two days, I think."

He glanced at the floor for a long moment, then nodded. "Okay. Where do you want me today? Back on the concession stand?"

"I know it's uncomfortable," she said. "I didn't know how to put her off without hurting her feelings."

"It's all right, Ames. I'm a big boy. I can handle it. Where do you want me?"

He didn't want to talk about it. Which made two of them.

"You've made a great start on the stand. So if you wanted to keep at it, that would be great."

"Sure." He exited to the foyer.

Amy closed her eyes for a long beat. If only she'd had the presence of mind to politely deflect Lisa's offer. And if only Lisa hadn't asked in the first place.

She'd made a start in the ladies' bathroom by the time Lisa arrived an hour later. Lisa struck a pose in the doorway, showing off what was obviously a brand-new pair of jeans and a crisp white T-shirt. "Check it out. The best Daylesford fashion has to offer. Good look for me, huh?"

She was being sarcastic since the jeans were about fifteen years out of date, but Lisa could make sackcloth look good.

"That T-shirt is going to stay clean for approximately sixty seconds. You know that, right?" Amy said, pushing her protective eye goggles up onto her forehead.

"Sacrifices have to be made. So, where do you want me?" Lisa rubbed her hands together as though she couldn't wait to dive into work.

Amy gestured toward the wall where she was scraping tile. "Grab a dust mask and some goggles and get banging. When we're done here, there's the gents' next door to tackle."

Amy had half expected Lisa to balk at the prospect of chipping tile off with a hammer and chisel, but she reached for the second pair of safety goggles without hesitation.

"Was Quinn okay about me helping out?" she asked after a short silence.

Amy hesitated a moment, wondering what her obligations were in this situation. Protect Lisa's feelings? Play peacekeeper?

"He wasn't exactly jumping for joy, but he's cool with it," she said, deciding simple honesty would have to do the trick.

A flicker of hurt crossed Lisa's face. Then she mustered a smile. "Well. I guess I should get used to that. So, am I just smashing the hell out of this stuff or is there an art to it?"

They worked side by side all morning. The tension banding Amy's chest slowly dissolved as she and Lisa caught up on each other's lives. It was uncomfortable hearing her friend talk about Stuart, the man she'd left Quinn for, but Amy figured she was going to have to get used to it if she and Lisa were to continue being friends. They were laughing about one of Lisa's court stories when Quinn appeared in the doorway.

"Lunch is up."

He didn't hang around for a response, slipping out the door and into the theatre. Amy tugged off her goggles and tried not to feel like a traitor because she'd been giggling with the enemy.

When she and Lisa entered the foyer they discovered Quinn had been out and bought rolls and doughnuts from the bakery, as well as large take-out coffees. He nudged the one marked low-fat toward Lisa wordlessly. She looked surprised for a moment before she took it and murmured a thank-you.

Amy watched them both surreptitiously as she ate her ham and salad roll. Ostensibly Quinn looked at ease, sprawled on the stairs, but she wondered if it was an act. Lisa kept up a steady stream of chatter about nothing much, a sure sign she was nervous. Amy swallowed the last bite of her roll as quickly as possible.

Not the most pleasant and relaxed meal of her lifetime, that was for sure.

She and Lisa went back to work once they'd polished off their doughnuts and by late afternoon they'd stripped all the walls bare.

"Coffee break," Amy declared as the last tile smashed to the floor. She sat back on her heels, dropped her hammer and chisel and shook out her aching arms.

"Isn't there a machine you can hire that can do this for you?" Lisa asked from the other side of the room.

She sounded exhausted and Amy spared her a glance. Her face was coated with dust and dirt and, as Amy had predicted, her T-shirt was beyond redemption.

"Probably, but I can't afford it," Amy said with a tired grin.

"I'll give you the money. Hell, I'll buy you the machine, no matter what it costs. Consider it a donation."

Amy pushed herself to her feet. "Come on. I'll buy you another one of those disgusting low-fat lattes you love so much and you'll feel better."

Quinn was working on the front panel of the counter when they passed. He glanced up at Amy when she rested a hand on his shoulder to get his attention but didn't turn the sander off. She mimed drinking a coffee and he nodded yes. Amy unlocked the front door and started walking toward the Gourmet Larder.

"I hope I haven't made things weird between you and Quinn," Lisa said after a moment.

Amy shot her a wary look. "What do you mean?"

"Well, it was just the two of you, before I came along. I'd hate to think I was cramping your style, making things weird between you both."

No worries about that. I took care of that all on my own.

"We're fine. Don't worry about it."

"I asked Quinn if he thought we could ever be friends again yesterday," Lisa volunteered suddenly.

Amy almost stumbled over a crack in the pavement. "What did he say?"

"That we can't turn back the clock."

Amy bit her lip and frowned at her feet. "Is that why you wanted to help out at the Grand? To try and change his mind?"

"No."

Amy slid her a look. Lisa's mouth tilted up at the corner.

"Okay, a little. But I wanted to help out, too. This way I get some bragging rights whenever I'm in town. 'I tiled the loos at the Grand.'"

They'd reached the Larder and Amy waited to one side as a woman with a baby pram exited the store. She was about to step over the threshold when someone called her name. She glanced over her shoulder and froze when she saw Barry Ulrich striding toward her.

"Shit."

"What's wrong?" Lisa asked.

"That's Barry Ulrich," Amy explained quietly.

She'd filled Lisa in on the developer's tactics over lunch and she felt Lisa straighten to her full height as Ulrich stopped in front of them. Thank God Lisa was a lawyer, too. Maybe she could stop Amy from making the situation even more disastrous than it already was.

"Ms. Parker. I was just coming to see you."

"I'm afraid I have nothing to say to you, Mr. Ulrich," Amy said coolly. "My lawyer has instructed me that any and all correspondence be directed through him."

Ulrich pulled an envelope from the leather portfolio he was carrying.

"I'm withdrawing the suit, so you can call off your guard dog, all right?" he said abruptly, offering her the envelope.

Amy stared at the letter but didn't take it. This had to be some kind of trick. Some ploy to get her mad enough to say something else stupid and destructive.

"Are you deaf or something? I said I'm dropping the action," Ulrich said impatiently.

No wonder she'd felt compelled to assault the man with a muffin—he was a rude butt-head.

"Let me," Lisa said, and she took the envelope. There was a rustle of paper as she unfolded the letter. After scanning it briefly she met Amy's eyes.

"It's true. He's filed a motion to drop the suit."

Amy felt a little dizzy. How…? Why…?

"I've done my bit, now it's time for you to do yours. Call off your guard dog," Ulrich said.

Amy shook her head, hopelessly lost and over-whelmed. "I don't know what you're talking about."

"Don't play games with me, missy. I've had two calls from the Australian Securities and Investment Commission this week already."

Amy opened her mouth to deny whatever he was accusing her of again but Lisa's hand suddenly clamped down on her shoulder.

"I assume this means Amy won't be having any more after-hours visitors at the theatre?" Lisa asked silkily.

Ulrich made a big deal out of straightening the cuffs on his shirt. "I don't know what you're talking about."

Lisa smiled thinly. "I'm afraid you're going to have to do better than that."

Ulrich glared at her for a long moment. Then he cleared his throat. "As far as I'm concerned, the Grand project is defunct. Ulrich Construction is no longer interested in the site."

Amy sucked in air to speak but Lisa's hand tightened on her shoulder again.

"Excellent. Pleasure doing business with you, Mr. Ulrich. Have a lovely day," Lisa said.

Amy gave in to the insistent pressure on her shoulder and started walking up the street, away from the Larder.

"What was that all about?" she asked when they were out of earshot. "Has he really dropped the suit? Is he trying to trick me or something?"

Lisa passed the letter over. "Read it yourself. He's acknowledged in writing that no material harm has come to him or his business as a result of your statements. Even if he wanted to, he can't sue you now. With that letter on record, it wouldn't get past a first meeting."

"But…why? I don't get it. He had me over a barrel. Quinn said he could keep me in court for years."

"One of the great things about being at law school with a bunch of other lawyers is the friendships you form," Lisa said. "All those study hours and parties after exams are great for bonding. Then you all graduate and go out into the big wide world. Some people end up in private practice, others go corporate. Others work for the government."

Lisa was walking so quickly Amy was struggling to keep up. In more ways than one.

"Okay, clearly I'm very thick, but I still don't get it," she said.

"One of the guys we studied with is at the Securities Commission," Lisa said. She shot Amy a loaded look.

Finally the pieces fell into place. "Quinn asked him to do a favor, and his friend turned up the heat on Ulrich," Amy guessed.

"That's right." Lisa's lips were thin.

A terrible thought occurred to Amy. She stopped in her tracks and grabbed Lisa's arm, forcing her to stop, too.

"What Quinn did…it's not going to get him into any trouble, is it?"

Why else would Lisa look so worried?

"I'm not going to lie to you. He's an officer of the court, Amy. If Ulrich makes a complaint saying that Quinn coerced him with the threat of reprisals, he could be disbarred for unethical behavior."

Which explained why Lisa was looking so grim.

"Oh, God."

What had Quinn been thinking? What kind of super-strength crazy pills had he been on to risk his entire career for her?

"Don't freak just yet, Ames. From what I saw back there, Ulrich's got too much to hide to risk putting in a complaint. Quinn's probably in the clear."

"But he should never have even thought about risking himself like that. I can't believe he would be so *stupid*."

"Yeah, well, there is that," Lisa said tightly. "If I thought he'd listen to me, I'd kick his ass from here to Melbourne and back for being such a cowboy."

Amy started walking again, head high, stride long. Lisa might hesitate to kick Quinn's ass, but she had no such compunction.

None at all.

Beneath her anger was a knee-knocking fear over what he might have brought on himself in her name.

"What are you going to do, Ames?" Lisa asked warily. She was the one puffing to keep up now.

"I'm going to kill him," Amy said between gritted teeth. "Then I'm going to resuscitate him and do it all over again."

QUINN WAS ON THE PHONE in the balcony section when Amy barreled through the archway from the upper foyer. Her face was set, her color high as she marched straight up to him, planted her hands on his chest and shoved so hard she knocked him off balance and forced him to take a step backward.

"You idiot!" she said, eyes blazing.

He blinked at her, vaguely aware that Lisa had followed her into the space.

"Listen, Justine, I'm going to have to call you back," he said into his phone. He ended the call and Amy took a threatening step toward him again, her index finger aimed at his chest now.

"How dare you take such a risk! How dare you do that in my name and not even consult me about it!" She punctuated each word with a painful stab of her finger into his sternum.

He grabbed her hand and held it immobilized between them.

"Will you calm down for a minute, you psycho chicken, and tell me what the hell is going on?"

Amy used her free hand to draw an envelope from her back pocket and slap it against his chest.

"*This* is what's going on. I cannot believe you did this and didn't even tell me about it."

Quinn saw the Ulrich Construction logo across the front of the envelope and went very still.

"What happened? What's he done now?"

"It's not what he's done, it's what you've done. He's withdrawn the suit. But you, you big bloody idiot, have risked your career to make it happen," Amy said, her voice strident with emotion.

The muscles in his belly and chest relaxed. "Thank Christ. You had me scared for a moment there."

"Don't you dare stand there and smile about it. Do you have any idea how furious I am with you right now?"

He caught Amy's other hand as she made a fist and aimed it at his chest. Any second now she was going to try to kick him in the shins.

His gaze found Lisa's over Amy's shoulder. He'd forgotten she was there.

"Would you mind giving us a bit of privacy?"

Lisa looked startled, as though she'd momentarily forgotten she no longer had front row seats to the big events in his life.

"Of course. Actually, Ames, I've got some calls I need to make…"

"No problem. I'll see you tomorrow," Amy said, even as she tried to jerk her arms free. "Will you let me go, please?"

Quinn waited until Lisa was gone. "If I let you go are you going to hit me again?"

"What do you think?"

"Then I'm not going to let you go."

She tugged on her arms one last time then gave up, glaring at him instead.

"I'm so angry with you. You have no idea. Why on

earth would you risk all those years of study—your partnership, for Pete's sake—for something so stupid?"

"The Grand isn't stupid. It's your dream."

"*My* dream, not yours. Where do you get off putting your life on the line for mine?"

He could hear the fear trembling beneath the indignation in her voice and he drew her closer.

"Ames. You're freaking over nothing. Ulrich's withdrawn the suit. Whatever worst-case-scenario you're imagining is not going to happen. It's okay."

"No, it's not. You shouldn't have done that without talking to me first. No way would I have ever asked you to take that kind of risk for me. You could have been disbarred!"

"Is that what Lisa told you? She's exaggerating."

"Look me in the eye and tell me it couldn't have happened."

He took a moment to compose his answer and she shook her head.

"Don't bother. I already know you're about to lie. You're the worst liar I ever met. It's a wonder you ever made it as a lawyer."

"I don't do a lot of trial work," he said, aiming for a humble, penitent tone. "Cuts down on the lying requirement."

"Don't try to weasel out of this by being cute. You think you did good, don't you? You think you're the champion of the hour."

"I wouldn't go that far. But you've got to admit, Ulrich dropping the suit is pretty good news."

"It's amazing news. But I'd rather lose the Grand altogether than have you get in trouble. You worked so hard to get that partnership. What were you thinking?"

"It's fine. I took a tiny risk, but it paid off. It's okay."

She stared at him for a long moment, then looked away.

"You could have at least told me what you were going to do. I should have had a vote on whether you threw away your law career for me or not."

"Next time. I promise," he said.

"There isn't going to be a next time. I'm never speaking to you again after this."

But she was smiling.

"Don't ever do something like that again, okay?" she said. "I want you to promise me."

Half her hair had escaped from her pigtails to bounce around her face. She looked incredibly pretty and fierce and dear to him as she waited for him to comply with her demand.

"I'm not going to lie to you, Ames. You'll only call me on it. If I had to do it again, I probably would."

A frown wrinkled her forehead as she gazed into his face. He reached out and rubbed his thumb along her cheekbone. Her skin was so soft.

"I'd do anything for you, Ames. You know that."

Something flared in her eyes, hot and needy, then she looked down. A muscle flickered in her jaw. When she looked up again the heat was gone, replaced with a wry expression.

"I should probably get that in writing. Could come in handy someday."

He frowned. Two days ago, he wouldn't have understood what had just happened. Wouldn't have had a clue that that little duck of her head had been about anything other than her ducking her head. But he knew how she felt now, what she wanted, and he knew he'd just witnessed her pushing all of her most private, passionate, secret emotions into a closet and kicking the door closed.

How many years had she been doing that? How many times had she swallowed the words she really wanted to say and replaced them with something funny and smart and completely not what was in her heart?

Too many.

Suddenly he saw the future stretching out in front of them, full of moments like this. Amy hiding her feelings, him pretending he hadn't noticed. Playing it safe. Hurting her because he was too scared of losing her.

It wasn't going to work. No way was it going to work. They couldn't pretend none of this had occurred. He couldn't even stand to be in the same room with her and not want to touch her—he'd proved as much in the past five minutes. They'd let the genie out of the bottle, and there was no way to stuff it back in. And as much as it scared the hell out of him, he didn't want to.

"Don't do that, Ames," he said quietly. "Don't hide from me like that. I can't stand it."

Her eyes were wide, startled. "Wh-what?"

He closed the distance between them and reached for her face, cupping her jaw in both his hands. He stared into her eyes, brushing his thumbs across her cheekbones. Then he lowered his mouth to hers.

For a long, hot second her lips softened and opened under his. He tasted her sweetness and had to fight the primitive, carnal urge to drag her to the floor. Then she tensed in his arms, arching her upper body away from him, pulling her face from his grasp.

"Quinn. Stop. What are you doing?"

"Kissing you. What does it look like?" He tried to kiss her again but she held him off.

"I thought we weren't doing this. I thought we'd decided it was a mistake."

"I know. For two smart people we can be pretty dumb sometimes."

He didn't give her a chance to say any more, simply lowered his head and kissed her. After a tense second her body softened and she made a small, helpless sound as her mouth opened beneath his.

Desire ripped through him. She felt so good. So right in his arms. Madness to think he would ever have been able to resist doing this again. Sheer madness.

Her hands clenched into his shoulder muscles and her whole body trembled as she strained closer. She wrapped a leg around his hip and rubbed herself shamelessly against his hard-on.

He wanted to push her against the wall and take her standing up. He wanted to tear her T-shirt off and lick and suck her breasts until she screamed for him to stop. He wanted to fulfill every one of the dirty, horny fantasies he'd forged in the darkened quiet of his bedroom when he was fourteen years old.

"Yoo-hoo! Anybody home?"

The sound of Mrs. Parker's voice echoed all the way up the staircase and across the upper foyer. Quinn closed his eyes and swore.

"You have got to be kidding. What the hell is with your mother and the drop-in visits?" he said.

Footsteps echoed in the main theatre as Mrs. Parker went on the hunt for them. He figured he had about sixty seconds before she came charging up here at exactly the wrong moment all over again.

He looked into Amy's face. "We need to talk."

She nodded. Then she licked her lips, a nervous little

dart of her tongue that made him want to drag her to a cave.

"I'll come over tonight, okay?" he said.

She nodded again. The dazed look had left her face and caution was creeping in to take its place. He kissed her again, hard.

"Don't worry."

He told himself it was a good thing that Mrs. P. had arrived as he walked away. If she hadn't, he wouldn't have been able to stop. And Amy deserved better than the cold, hard floor of the balcony section.

If they were going to do this, they were going to do it right. And if they weren't…well, that was a conversation for tonight, as well.

AMY HEARD Quinn greet her mother on the stairs. Her heart was pounding so loudly it was a miracle it hadn't jumped right out of her chest. She pressed her hand over it, just in case.

Quinn had kissed her. And he was coming over tonight. To talk.

"Oh my God," she whispered. "Oh my God."

Her mother's footsteps sounded across the upper foyer and she made an effort to compose herself. If she kept standing here gaping like a stunned mullet her mother would take one look at her and know, same as last time. And there was no way Amy wanted to talk about Quinn right now. Not while she was still trying to come to terms with his kiss and what it meant.

She turned and picked up a paint roller and started ripping the protective plastic sleeve off it.

"Mom. Hey," she said supercasually as her mother walked beneath the archway a few seconds later.

"There you are. I came to tell you that your father got you a good deal on two-pack polyurethane for the floors. He wanted to know how much you thought you'd need so he can put it aside."

"Yeah? That's fantastic. What sort of discount are we talking?"

It took an effort to put her business cap on, but Amy managed it. She talked sensibly and rationally for twenty minutes. She nodded and commented in all the appropriate places. Then she locked the door behind her mother and it hit her all over again.

Quinn.

The kiss.

Him coming over tonight.

Her knees turned to jelly thinking about it. After sixteen years, was it possible that he was going to…? That they were going to…? That this was real?

She closed her eyes, sending up a little prayer to whoever oversaw these kinds of situations.

Please, please, please let me not have the wrong end of the stick. Please let this be what I think it is.

Then she broke into a run as she headed for the rear exit. She hadn't shaved her legs for weeks. As for her bikini line… Suffice to say, it had been a while. Then there was her bedroom, a mess of abandoned clothes and tangled sheets and breeding dust bunnies.

She checked her watch as she slid into her car. It was nearly five. Quinn had said he'd come over *tonight*. Did that mean six, or seven? Maybe it meant eight? If it was six, she was screwed. Utterly. And she was wasting valuable leg-shaving time staring out her windshield. She slammed the key into the ignition and started the car.

It wasn't until she was tearing the sheets off her bed

that she remembered Lisa. Which went to show how far gone she was.

She sank onto the bed.

The last thing she wanted to do was hurt Lisa. Yes, her friend had made some ill-judged, self-destructive decisions, but that did not make her any less Amy's friend. If something happened with Quinn tonight, if he came over and they talked and…whatever…Lisa was going to be upset. She'd feel as though Amy had simply been hovering in the wings all these years, waiting to take Lisa's place by Quinn's side.

And, in a way, she'd be right.

But she'd also be wrong, because Amy would never have tried to oust Lisa. She might have stood with envy in her heart at Quinn and Lisa's wedding, but she'd celebrated, too. She'd been happy for them, even as she'd longed for things she'd thought she could never have.

If Lisa were still with Quinn, none of this would be happening. With a certainty. Quinn would never have betrayed Lisa, and Amy would never have tried to seduce him away from her friend.

But Quinn and Lisa were getting a divorce. And Quinn had kissed Amy. He wanted her. She allowed herself to believe it, remembering the way he'd held her. She didn't know how deep his feelings ran, if it was simply attraction or much more, but she very badly wanted to find out. God, how she wanted to find out.

She put her head in her hands. If she pursued her heart's desire, there was a very real chance she would lose her friendship with Lisa. Was that a price she was prepared to pay?

She thought about all the memories she and Lisa shared. And she thought about Quinn, about her enduring, bone-deep love for him. She thought about the future, about babies and houses and growing old beside the man she loved.

Maybe it made her selfish, maybe she was buying herself bad karma to last several lifetimes, but she loved Quinn. She was going to grab on to this chance for happiness with both hands and hang on. Lisa had had her chance and she'd made her choices. She would have to live with them, as Amy would have to live with hers.

Standing, she bundled the dirty sheets together. She needed to find her good underwear.

QUINN ANGLED HIS JAW and shaved the last of his five-o'clock shadow. He took a step back from the vanity and checked his hair.

There was a goofy bit sticking up at the back and he smoothed it with his fingers. It resisted the hint and sprang up again.

He checked his watch. Nearly six-thirty. He needed to get going. While he was primping in the bathroom like a nervous teenager, Amy was waiting for him.

He grabbed his toothbrush and started brushing furiously. He leaned forward to have another go at the goofy bit with his free hand and groaned as toothpaste dripped down the front of his shirt.

"Bloody hell."

He grabbed a towel and scrubbed at the mark but a faint white outline remained on his dark shirt.

"Great. Well done."

Maybe he should change shirts. He looked at his watch again. It would take him ten minutes to drag out the ironing board and press another shirt.

Too long. Way too long.

Amy would have to put up with him in all his tooth-paste-spotted glory. She'd seen him looking far worse, he figured.

He hustled to the kitchen and started loading up a carrier bag with the supplies he'd bought earlier. Brie, check. Pricey bottle of pinot noir, check. Gourmet crackers, spicy pear paste, antipasto, check.

He was showered, ironed, after-shaved and loaded to the hilt with fancy foodstuffs. He figured he was about as ready as he was ever going to be.

He reached for his car keys and saw that his hands were trembling.

Damn.

He let out his breath on a gust and braced his hands on the kitchen counter.

Okay. He needed to calm down. This was Amy, after all. His best friend. Whatever happened tonight, they could deal with it.

He grabbed his keys and strode for the door. If he hung around thinking for too long, he'd psyche himself out. He'd made his decision this afternoon. He wanted Amy. He loved her. He was going to take the risk.

He threw open the front door and nearly walked straight into Lisa. She had her hand raised, ready to knock, and she made a surprised sound when she saw him.

"Oh. You scared me."

"Lisa. I was just on my way out."

Her gaze took in his freshly ironed shirt and damp hair before dropping to the carrier bag in his hand.

"I only need five minutes."

"Can't it wait?"

"I don't think so, no."

There was a low, emotional note to her voice. Quinn checked his watch again and took a step backward. "Five minutes."

Not exactly gracious, but they were past the point of playing polite games with each other.

And Amy was waiting.

Lisa swept past him in a swirl of jasmine and spice, walking into the living room. He followed more slowly and stopped when she turned to face him.

Her shoulders rose as she took a deep breath. "I've been trying to work out why I felt so compelled to come down here. At first I thought it was about Amy, and our friendship. But then I realized…I want a second chance, Quinn."

Her words hung in the air for what felt like a long time. He bent his knees and put the carrier bag down.

Five minutes, his ass.

"Why?" he asked bluntly.

"Isn't it obvious? I still love you."

"What about what's-his-name?"

"Stuart and I broke up three months ago."

That surprised him.

"You can't just slot back into your old life, Lisa. It doesn't work like that."

"I don't expect us to pick things up where we left off. I know I've hurt you. Betrayed your trust. I've been seeing a counselor, and I think I understand myself a little better now. I want to make it up to you."

"Lisa." He stopped and ran a hand through his hair. Until a few minutes ago, his head had been filled with nothing but Amy. He'd been thinking about the future, about what might be. And now Lisa was standing here, offering an alternative.

"We'll take it slowly. We can date. Get to know each

other again." She took a step toward him and he belatedly saw he wasn't the only one who'd dressed to impress this evening.

His gaze ran over her figure-hugging red dress and very high heels. She'd even worn her hair up, the way she knew he liked it.

"You've been gone a year," he said. Three, if he counted the two years she'd been sneaking around behind his back. And he did.

"I know you're angry with me. You have every right to be. But I understand so much more now, Quinn. My parents, the way they've always been with me, nothing ever being good enough or big enough or bright enough to get their attention. I've been busting my ass for years trying to get them to notice me. And they still don't give a shit. And I've managed to ruin the one good and perfect thing in my life trying to prove to myself that I'm worthy of being loved."

She clutched her hands together at her waist.

"I screwed up, Quinn. I was looking in all the wrong places for things to make me whole. Please, please give us another chance. I miss you so much."

She was offering him answers to the questions that had haunted him, and she was offering him a way to right the biggest, most abject failure of his life.

A year ago—hell, six months ago—he'd have leaped at the opportunity. He'd have swallowed his pride and reined in his anger and done his best to salvage what he could from her betrayal.

Lisa gave a choked sob and pressed a hand to her mouth. "I'm too late, aren't I? God, I'm too late."

She started to cry, big, noisy, wrenching sobs, her shoulders hunched as though she could somehow contain her grief if she could only make herself small enough.

He hesitated a moment, then stepped forward and pulled her into his arms. She clutched at him, pressing her face into his neck, her body shuddering against his.

"I don't want to lose you. I don't want to lose you," she said over and over.

It had been more than a year since he'd held her. He was surprised at how comfortable she felt in his arms. In her high heels she was almost as tall as him. So different from Amy in so many ways.

He stood breathing in her perfume and felt the tug of shared history and emotion dragging at him. Not so many years ago, he'd stood before a priest and made promises to her. Promises he'd had every intention of keeping.

"I don't want to lose you," Lisa said.

She sounded so broken, so helpless. He slid his hand to the back of her neck.

"It's okay," he said. "It's okay."

CHAPTER ELEVEN

BY SEVEN-THIRTY AMY had paced the hallway so many times she could do it blindfolded. Ten steps to the door, swivel on heel, ten steps to the living room, swivel on heel.

Repeat.

Endlessly.

Where the hell was Quinn?

She'd thought about phoning him, but what was she supposed to say? "I still love you, what's keeping you?" She figured she'd made herself vulnerable enough in this situation as it was.

Maybe he'd chickened out. Maybe she'd scared the hell out of him with her desperate neediness when he kissed her and she wrapped her leg around his waist and held on to him like a limpet on a log.

Maybe he'd simply changed his mind.

Maybe he'd had a car accident driving the three blocks to her house.

Maybe he'd hopped the first flight back to Sydney.

By a quarter to eight she had so many excuses and re-criminations circling her mind she was seriously consid-ering banging her head against the wall just to clear it.

"Damn you, Quinn. Don't you dare do this to me!"

She grabbed her car keys. Enough was enough. She

was going to find out what was holding him up. And if it was nothing, if he was sitting at home twiddling his thumbs while she gnawed her fingernails down to stumps and wore a groove in her front hallway…well, he was going to be walking funny for a while, that was for sure.

Her hands were tight on the steering wheel as she drove to his street. She turned into Lavender Lane and her parents' house came up on her right. She slowed the car.

Then she saw it. Shiny and sleek and black. Lisa's car, parked in Quinn's driveway behind his rental sedan.

Right.

Of course.

She braked and stared at Lisa's personalized plate for a long minute, the engine of her rusty heap idling noisily.

She should have known. And maybe, on some subconscious level, she had. Which was why she'd waited so long before she got in the car and drove over here.

She drove home and slammed the car door so loudly the neighbor's cat bolted for cover, his night-eyes glinting brightly. She stalked up the path and shoved the door open, hearing it smash into the hall wall with a satisfying crash.

She was an idiot. A very foolish, very naive, self-deluded idiot.

She could see it so clearly now. Talk about twenty-twenty hindsight. All the years she'd spent mooning after Quinn, loving him in silence—wasted, every one. All the energy she'd expended over the past few days anguishing about kissing him and confessing to him—a huge waste.

Because Quinn Whitfield was never going to love her the way she loved him.

She'd said it to herself a hundred, maybe even a

thousand times. But until this moment she'd never truly believed it. Not even when she'd blurted her feelings to him two nights ago and he'd simply stared blankly at her. Even then, faced with his lack of reaction, she'd still had a chink of hope in her pathetic, needy heart.

But not now. Tonight she had reached the end of her rope.

Sure, Quinn might want to kiss her. He might even be curious about sleeping with her. He might feel touched by her confession and obligated to do something about it.

But he would never feel the same way about her as he did about Lisa.

It had always been the two of them. Lisa and Quinn, Quinn and Lisa. From the first summer when the two of them had gotten together, Amy had always been the one on the outside looking in. And she still was.

They'd been *married,* for God's sake. They'd woken to each other's morning breath thousands of times. They'd shared intimacies she couldn't even imagine. She could never compete with that.

"Done. I'm done," she told her house.

She waited for the sky to fall, the earth to quake. Loving Quinn had been so much a part of her world that washing her hands of it felt akin to kicking the earth out of its orbit around the sun.

But nothing happened. Her hall clock ticked away another few seconds of her life. The neighbor's dog barked. Her heart kept pumping blood and other vital matter around her body.

So.

Life went on.

How about that.

Her mouth firmed. She could do this. Get over Quinn. Move on, finally. She bloody could.

Then her gaze fell on an old photograph resting on her hall table: her and Quinn at nine years old, riding their bikes past her parents' place, the two of them dressed as jockeys to celebrate Melbourne Cup day.

She reached out and pushed the frame over so that it fell facedown on the table. The last thing she needed to be looking at right now was a reminder of how entwined her life was with his.

She walked two steps and found herself staring at another picture, this one a Picasso print. Quinn had bought it for her for her eighteenth birthday. And next to it was another photograph: her mom standing with Louise Whitfield, both of them holding colorful cocktails high in a toast.

Amy stared at the Picasso for a long moment. She'd hung it opposite her bedroom door so she could see it when she was in bed. It was one of the first things she saw every morning. And every time she looked at it, she thought of Quinn.

Heat pressed at the back of her eyes. She screwed up her face, breathing deeply. She would not cry. She wouldn't. She'd cried so many times over the years. But not tonight.

Please, not tonight. If she started, she was afraid she might never stop.

For a moment she teetered on the brink...and then the moment of danger passed. She sniffed loudly, blinked a few times.

Okay. All right. Good. Keep moving. Hold on to the anger.

She strode into the study and shifted things around until she'd found a large box. She brought it to the hall and grabbed the photograph off the table and put it in the box. Then she added the Picasso print and the other photograph. She went into her bedroom next. In went the silk robe Lisa and Quinn had bought her for Christmas three years ago. The earrings Quinn had given her last time she'd been in Sydney. Her ancient Midnight Oil tour T-shirt, bought when she and Quinn drove into Melbourne and braved the crowds to get front row seats.

Anything that reminded her of him. Anything that might keep her anchored in the past. Because she was done, and she was not going to waste another second of her life wanting someone who would never be hers.

She was thirty years old. Still young. Somewhere out there in the world was a man who would love her the way she deserved to be loved, a man she could love freely, without guilt and complications.

She looked around her bedroom.

She was going to need another box.

THE FRONT DOOR WAS OPEN when Quinn climbed the steps to Amy's porch. Light streamed out into the night as he stopped in the doorway.

"Ames?" The carrier bag rustled against his legs.

It was nearly eight-thirty. He'd called the moment he'd closed the door on Lisa, but Amy hadn't picked up.

He stepped into the house.

"Amy? It's me."

There was a carton in the hallway, filled with picture frames and clothes and other household items. He recognized the Picasso print he'd given Amy on her eighteenth birthday and the stuffed turtle he'd won for her at the Royal Melbourne Show one year.

Amy rounded the corner at the other end of the hallway, another box in her arms. Her step faltered when she saw him, then her chin came up and she strode up the hallway and dumped her burden next to the first box.

"Sorry I'm late," he said. He raised the bag of food and wine. "I bought some stuff."

"I'm taking it back," she said coolly, her gaze steady. "I want you to forget I ever said it."

He frowned. "Taking what back?"

"The *I love you*. I'm taking it back. Retracting it, as you lawyers would say. So there's no need for us to have this little chat."

She crossed her arms over her breasts. He didn't think he'd ever seen her so angry.

"Ames. I'm sorry I took so long to get here. Lisa came over and—"

"I know. I got sick of waiting so I came to you. Anyway. I have stuff to do, so if you don't mind, I'll get back to it."

She turned and walked down the hallway. Quinn followed, glancing into the second box as he passed. The pencil case he'd made in woodwork in Year 9 was sitting on top of a pile of Raymond Chandler books. All of which he'd bought for her when they'd both fallen in love with Chandler's writing when they were in their early twenties.

He followed her into the living room and watched as she started sorting through her CD collection, tossing unwanted albums into yet another box. He didn't need to look to know that they were all albums that he'd either bought for her or that they both enjoyed.

"Lisa and I aren't getting back together, Ames," he said quietly.

"I didn't think you were."

He frowned. "Then what's going on?"

"Nothing's going on." She paused, then shook her head. "No, that's not true. Something is going on, it's just nothing to do with you."

She went back to sorting through her CDs.

An icy finger of fear slid down his spine. He didn't understand what was going on. He'd never seen her like this. So shut off, so cold.

He dumped the wine and food on her coffee table and crossed the room, tugging the pile of CDs from her hands.

"Talk to me."

"There's nothing to say."

She reached for the CDs but he threw them onto her couch where they landed with a plastic clatter. They were both silent for a long moment, then she lifted her face and looked him in the eye.

"You said you'd come over tonight to talk. You kissed me and you said you'd be here. Then you left me hanging."

"I know. I'm sorry. I literally walked into Lisa on my doorstep as I was leaving to come here. She wanted to talk, wouldn't take no for an answer. She was upset—"

"I don't care," Amy said. "It doesn't matter. In fact, it's probably good tonight happened. It made a few things very clear to me."

She tried to brush past him but he grabbed her shoulders. She went very still.

"Don't touch me."

"Ames—"

"No. I don't want to hear it, okay? I get it. I finally get it. And I don't want your pity or your curiosity or whatever it is. I don't want to be second best or your consolation prize or an afterthought. *I deserve better.*"

There were so many things wrong with what she was saying that he didn't know where to begin.

"If you would listen to me for five seconds—"

"It doesn't matter, Quinn. Nothing you say is going to change anything. This was never going to work. I've spent half my life loving you, and you've been married to someone else for six years. One of these things is not like the other. You're never going to feel the same way as me. How could you?"

He wanted to shake her till the angry, empty look left her face. He wanted to yell his denial till the rafters shook and the windows rattled. Instead, he tightened his grip on her shoulders and jerked her body against his.

"You have no freakin' idea how I feel, Amy Parker."

Then he kissed her. Not gently or tenderly or patiently, the way he'd planned. There was no wine and cheese and fine words and promises. Just her mouth beneath his, her body against his, as he kissed her with all the frustration and passion and need and fear in him. Her hands came up to grasp his shoulders and for a moment he thought she was going to try to push him away. Then she wrapped her arms around him and slid her tongue along his and pressed her hips forward, straining to get as close to him as possible.

He slid a hand down her shoulder to find her breast, palming it, rubbing her nipple with his thumb. She retaliated by grabbing his backside and pressing herself against his hard-on. He groaned and she slid a hand around his waist and into the waistband of his jeans. He broke their kiss to jerk her T-shirt up and push her bra down, tugging her nipple into his mouth. Her body jerked as he bit her nipple then soothed it with his tongue. She yanked his fly down and slid her hand inside his boxer briefs, wrapping her fingers around his erection. She stroked his length, once, twice, three times. He backed her toward the couch and pushed her down. They hit the cushions together and the couch jerked as one of the front legs gave with a sharp crack, sending them tumbling onto the floor. His elbow hit the coffee table and Amy's head thunked against his.

"Are you okay?" he asked, reaching out to touch her face.

Her eyes were glazed, her cheeks flushed. "Yes." She grasped his shoulders and pushed him onto his back and climbed on top of him.

He dragged her T-shirt the rest of the way off and reached for the clasp on her bra. She started peeling his jeans off and he lifted his hips obligingly. She made a small, needy sound as his erection sprang free and he lost it for a moment, grabbing her and kissing her so hard that their teeth clashed and they bumped noses. Her hands kept working at his jeans all the while, tugging them down his thighs then pushing them over his knees. He kicked himself free and reached for the stud on her jeans. Amy made an impatient noise and rolled to one side, unzipping her fly and sticking her thumbs into the waistband of her jeans, shucking them in one frantic, urgent motion. The moment she was naked he rolled on top of her, grunting when his shoulder connected with the coffee table. She opened her thighs wide and he groaned again as his hips settled against hers and his erection nudged into her moist heat. She wrapped her legs around his hips and arched her back.

They were both gasping like landed fish, mindless, mad. He pressed his hips forward, greedy for more, wanting everything.

And somewhere in the back of his mind a thought

flickered to life. He stilled and looked down into Amy's hectic face.

"Condom," he said shortly.

She frowned as though she didn't understand what language he was speaking, then she shook her head. "I'm on the pill."

Her hands found his ass and urged him closer but the small moment of clarity had already led to a greater moment.

This was Amy. And he was about to shag her on the floor of her house with no finesse and very little thought beyond the quickest way to get her naked.

"Bed. We should be in a bed," he said.

"I don't care."

"I do. I want this to be special. This is our first time."

"Our first time," she repeated.

"Yes."

She smiled, a tremulous, hopeful, heartbreaking smile.

"I guess we should make an effort, then. My bedroom's the first doorway on the right."

They disengaged as though someone had fired a starting pistol, scrambling to their feet and hotfooting it up the hallway.

She stopped in her tracks when they entered her bedroom, a dismayed expression on her face. "No sheets. I was so busy shaving my legs and finding my good underwear I forgot to finish making the bed."

"Are you kidding? Who cares about sheets?" he said, and he took her to the mattress in a flying tackle.

They butted noses again as they kissed, her breasts warm against his chest, her legs tangling with his. Then she was spreading her thighs wide and he was nudging at her entrance and—finally—sliding inside her.

They both froze, the room suddenly very quiet. He looked into her face and saw the need and wonder and truth in her eyes and wondered if she saw the same in his.

"Amy," he said, lowering his forehead to press it against hers. "Amy."

Her arms came around him and locked tight.

"Quinn. Whatever you do, don't you dare stop now or I will be forced to kill you."

He laughed, couldn't help it. Need took over and he flexed his hips and withdrew. Then he slid into her all over again and she dropped her head back and made a low, needy humming sound in the back of her throat.

Sixteen years.

Unbelievable, but it might just have been worth the wait.

AMY FELT Quinn's backside flex beneath her hands as he bore down on her. Hot, hard strength filled her, stretching her. She forgot to breathe.

She'd wanted this for so long. Too long.

Quinn inside her, surrounding her. A part of her.

Then he found his rhythm and lust rose to swamp everything except sensation as he stroked into her, over and over. She rode with him, circling her hips to find the most satisfying friction. Clutching at his hard, beautiful body. Savoring every hitch in his breath, every brush of his hands against her breasts, her belly, her hips. Breathing and sighing and whispering his name.

Tension bowed her body. He kissed her breasts, licked her nipples, murmured things against her skin. She strained toward him, wanting everything he had to give.

And then she was there, her climax crashing down on her. She lost all sense of time. She'd barely come down to earth again when he tensed, pressing his face into her neck. He breathed her name over and over as he came, his body shuddering against hers.

Afterward, he lay heavy and lax on her for a long moment, his ragged breath warm against her neck. After a while he withdrew and rolled to the side, taking her with him. They lay facing each other and she ran her fingers through the dark silk of his chest hair, reveling in the freedom to touch him.

"I'm sorry I was late, Ames. Believe me, if it had been up to me, I would have been here at six-thirty."

She met his eyes. "She wanted to get back with you, didn't she?"

"How did you know?"

"It's not rocket science."

He brushed his hand over her shoulder, skimmed his knuckles along the curve of her jaw.

"She was upset. And for the first time I clued in that if something happened between us she was going to be even more upset. So I told her."

Amy tensed. "You told her? About us? But we hadn't even… I mean, we'd barely even…"

"Ames, we've practically torn each other's clothes off twice in as many days. I figured it was a pretty safe bet."

"Hmph." She concentrated on tracing the smooth arc of his pec muscle for a moment. "Was she okay? I mean, how did she react?"

"She was pretty emotional. I explained that there was no going back for us. She said she understood that part but she couldn't get her head around the two of us together. She wanted to know how long I'd felt this way, if anything had ever happened between the two of us before."

"What did you tell her?"

"The truth, Ames. That when we were married I only ever allowed myself to think of you as my friend."

She nodded. "Good. Because I would never have done that to her."

"I think she knows that. But she's working her way through a lot of stuff right now. It took a while to talk about things."

He reached out and tucked a stray curl behind her ear. "I'm sorry I kept you waiting."

"It's okay."

"Yeah?"

"Yeah. You're here now. That's the important bit."

He smiled at her, the corners of his eyes crinkling. He looked so familiar and so sexy lying beside her.

"Pinch me," she said. "I still can't quite believe this is real."

"I can do better than that."

He rolled toward her and slid a long, muscly leg over both of hers. His hand cupped her breast and she closed her eyes as he teased her nipple with his thumb and forefinger.

"You're so beautiful, Ames."

He lowered his head to her breasts, kissing the soft curve before opening his mouth over her nipple and rasping the rough of his tongue against her sensitive flesh. She opened her eyes and looked down at his dark head against her pale skin, watched him sucking and kissing her. She drove her fingers into his hair and held him close, running the sole of her foot along one of his strong calves. He had a wonderful body, strong and muscular, hairy in all the right places, unashamedly masculine.

He lifted his head and skimmed his hand down her ribs to her hip, his eyes following the movement.

"So soft…" He trailed his hand down her thigh and nudged her knee to one side. She caught her breath as he began to trail his fingers up the inside of her thigh. He shifted in the bed so that he could press a kiss against her belly.

"You know, when we were fourteen I used to watch you get changed from my bedroom window. When you had your blind down and the bedside lamp on I could see everything in silhouette. Well, almost everything. It used to drive me crazy." He said it lazily, casually, his focus on her body.

She frowned. "It's okay. You don't have to whisper sweet nothings in my ear."

"Sweet nothings. Was that what I was doing?"

"You don't have to tell me what you think I want to hear."

He lifted his head and shifted onto one elbow. "You think I'm making it up? You don't believe I used to lie in the dark watching you take off your bra and pull down your panties and feel like the dirtiest, filthiest little pervert under the sun because of all the things I wanted to do to you?"

She shifted uncomfortably. "I know I said a bunch of stuff before about being second best and a consolation prize. It's okay. You don't have to try to prove anything to me or make me feel better. Let's just…be here. This is enough," she said.

And it was. It was more than she'd ever thought she'd have from him.

He looked arrested. "You really don't believe me, do you?"

"I was there that summer, too, Quinn. I remember Lisa and her tiny red bikini."

He sat up suddenly. "Get dressed," he said, swinging his feet over the side of the bed.

"Sorry?"

"Get dressed. There's something I want to show you."

"But—"

He was already gone, padding down the hallway toward the living room. She grabbed the nearest T-shirt and tugged it on. Quinn was pulling his jeans on when she entered the living room.

"Where are we going? I don't get it," she said.

"Exactly." He bent and picked up her jeans, tossing them to her. "Get dressed, Ames."

There was a determined, stubborn note to his voice that she recognized. Frowning, she located her panties in the leg of her jeans. Quinn reached across and plucked them from her hands before she could pull them on.

"You won't be needing those. Do you still have that flashlight in your handbag?"

Five minutes later, they were in Quinn's car. Amy was acutely aware that she was commando and that she still had no idea where he was taking her.

"This thing you're showing me, it isn't in a public place, is it?" she asked nervously.

He signaled as they approached her parents' street and turned, stopping in front of their house.

"What are we doing here?" she asked stupidly.

"I'll show you."

He rounded the car and took her hand. He flicked the flashlight on, then led her up the driveway. Bluish light flickered behind the blinds in the living room, indicating her parents were still up watching television. Quinn led her past the window and into the backyard. The decorative gate between her mother's vegetable garden and the more unruly bottom half of the yard squeaked in protest as he opened it.

"Okay, this is getting weird," she said. "Why are we in my parents' backyard?"

Quinn didn't say anything, simply led her to the very bottom of the garden, into the long, damp grass where they used to play in years gone by. The flashlight beam slid over the grass and settled on the gnarled trunk of the apple tree.

"Hold the light steady for me, okay?" he said.

Bemused, she took the flashlight and aimed the beam at the tree trunk as he hauled himself up onto a low branch and began to climb.

"You're crazy, you know that, right?" she said.

"Maybe. It's been a long time. It's probably— Hah! Look at that. Guess I must be a better craftsman than I thought. Throw me the flashlight and come up here."

Muttering under her breath, Amy tossed him the flashlight, the beam arcing through the night as it flew through the air. Quinn trained the light down the trunk and she swung herself up into the tree. He hadn't climbed very far, about halfway into the canopy. He was straddling a thick branch and she settled in beside him, one hand grasping an overhead branch for balance.

Quinn aimed the flashlight at the tree trunk. "Take a look."

She glanced at him, then turned to study the rough, gray bark. It was well hidden, camouflaged by years of weather, but she could make out the faint outline of a love heart carved into the wood. Two sets of initials had been carved inside it. She reached out to trace them with her fingertip.

"'Q.W. 4 A.P.,'" she read. She stared at Quinn, stunned. "How long has this been here?"

"We turned fourteen in ninety-four, right? So I guess it's been here sixteen years."

She stared at him. All these years she'd looked for proof that her feelings for Quinn were reciprocated. And all the time it had been right here in her parents' backyard.

She reached out and pressed her hand against the rough bark. For a moment she was overwhelmed. Then she swung around and scrambled down the tree.

Quinn dropped to the ground beside her a few seconds later.

"I don't understand," she said after a short silence. "Why didn't you ever say anything?"

"Why didn't you?" he countered.

"Because I was afraid. Because if I did say something and you didn't feel the same, things would have been weird between us."

"Ditto. You were my best friend, Ames. I didn't want to lose you."

"But you were happy to lose Lisa. She was your friend, too."

As soon as she said it she wished it back. She sounded so small and jealous.

"Not happy, but less uncomfortable, definitely. You and I grew up together. Lisa was one of the musketeers, but she wasn't like you. You and I had serious history. The kind of history that made me want to wash my brain out with soap every time I watched you get undressed. The truth is, if she hadn't made the first move, I probably would have stuck to hitting on the girls at school."

"Lisa made the first move?"

"That's right."

Amy thought back to that afternoon by the lake when Lisa had revealed what had happened the previous night with Quinn.

"Lisa told me you kissed her while you were doing your French homework," she said slowly. "She said you made the first move."

A frown creased Quinn's forehead. "The French homework part is right, but she was the one who jumped me. As far as I was concerned, the two of you were off-limits."

Amy stared at him. She didn't know why what he'd just said made such a difference to her, but it did. She felt as though something painful that had long been out of place had shifted back into alignment inside her.

Then she knew what it was. All these years, she'd thought Quinn had chosen Lisa over her. But Lisa was the one who'd done the choosing.

It was a small but important distinction for Amy.

"Have you ever seen that movie *Sliding Doors?*" she asked.

"Does it have explosions and chicks in bikinis toting guns?"

She gave him a dry look. "It's about the life you could have had if you made different choices."

"Ah." He was silent for a moment, then he brushed a hand down her arm. "Great idea for a movie."

"But?"

He shrugged. "Real life is more complicated."

She understood what he was saying with those few, spare words: he'd loved Lisa. He'd married her, been prepared to build forever with her. He wasn't going to say he regretted any of that as a sop to Amy. He was too honest for that.

She caught his hand in hers. If he'd felt any other way, she'd like him a lot less than she did. And she liked him a whole hell of a lot.

He pulled her into his arms. She closed her eyes and savored the closeness and the promise.

After a few minutes, Quinn cleared his throat.

"You know how I mentioned those dirty, horny, perverted fantasies I used to have?" he said. "One of them involved this particular bit of your parents' yard and all this long grass."

"Really?"

"To my shame."

He didn't look very ashamed.

"Is that why you wouldn't let me put my underwear on?"

"I like to plan ahead."

"Pretty confident, aren't you?"

He kissed her deeply, pushing her back against the old apple tree, holding her there with his hips and his flat belly. She shivered as his hands slid under her T-shirt to cup her braless breasts. He kissed her neck, then nuzzled the sensitive place beneath her ear. She slid her hands under his T-shirt and smoothed her hands across his back and chest and belly before finally finding the stud on his jeans and working it free.

One day, she would take the time to explore his body slowly and surely. But not tonight. Tonight she was too impatient, too needy, too desperate.

They sank to their knees in the grass and Quinn pulled his T-shirt off and spread it on the ground to protect her from the damp grass.

"So gallant," she said as he eased her onto her back.

"Smart mouth."

Suddenly the light came on at the back of her parents' house, flooding the yard.

"Is there somebody out there? Amy, is that you?" her mother called.

"No. Tell me this isn't happening." Quinn rested his

forehead against hers. "Has she got a wiretap on you or something? I swear, she's like a walking hard-on detector."

Amy bit her lip, trying not to laugh. Quinn levered himself up on his arms.

"Mrs. P., if you value your life, you'll go back inside and turn off the light right now."

"Quinn? Is that you?" Her mother's footsteps sounded on the patio as she came to investigate. "What on earth are you doing out there in the middle of the night?"

Amy stuffed her hand into her mouth.

"Well, I was kind of hoping to get your daughter naked. Then I was planning on spending the rest of my life making her happy," Quinn said. "If that's okay with you and Mr. P."

There was a short silence, then the sound of her mother's footsteps retreating. After a few seconds the light went off.

Quinn settled his weight over her again. "Now, where were we?"

"You were living out your teen fantasy."

"That's right."

But instead of finishing undressing her, his expression suddenly became very serious. He traced the angle of her jaw, brushed his thumb over her lips, pressed a kiss to her forehead.

"All these years... I love you, Ames. I can't imagine my life without you in it. I never want to lose you."

Amy stared into his face, so well known and precious to her. She thought about all the challenges that still lay ahead—working things out with Lisa, if that was even possible, the fact that Quinn's hard-earned partnership was in Sydney and she was bound to the Grand, plus all the small, everyday complications any two people faced when trying to build a future together.

"Then don't," she said.

EPILOGUE

Eight months later

"THIS SUIT IS HOT. And scratchy. Tell me again how you talked me into wearing this?" Quinn said.

Amy stifled a smile as she looked at the man in the gorilla suit standing next to her. Any second now the first guests would arrive for the official opening ceremony for the restored Grand Picture Theatre. The invitation had asked guests to come as their favorite stars of the silver screen. In keeping with their own theme, she and Quinn had paid a visit to the costume rental shop.

They were expecting over three hundred guests tonight, many of them Quinn's clients from his new practice. He had a shopfront on Vincent Street and more than enough work to keep him busy and challenged. There was the case he'd taken on last month, for instance—a negligence action against a certain property developer. Pro bono, naturally.

"You're the one who insisted on being King Kong to my Fay Wray. You said that it was one of the greatest love stories of all time," she said.

"There was a very real chance that I was under the influence of powerful pheromones and hormones at the time as a result of our honeymoon. Someone should have stepped in and saved me from myself."

She reached up and patted his furry face. "You make a very sexy primate, if it's any consolation."

He made a jungle noise in the back of his throat and wrapped a big, furry arm around her, pulling her against his chest.

"Me want pretty lady."

"Me want sweaty, scratchy monkey."

"Help me get this head off so I can kiss you," Quinn said.

She heard the sound of voices and high heels click-clacking on the tiled foyer.

"Too late. We're on."

There were waiters and waitresses in the foyer with trays of champagne and wine, but she and Quinn should really be there to greet their guests. She couldn't wait to celebrate their achievements with their friends and family. Quinn's parents had taken a break from their adventures on the road to attend. And Lisa had flown in this morning.

Although she'd been invited, Lisa hadn't come to their wedding. Amy had understood, but she'd still felt the loss. There had been a few e-mails exchanged since then, a couple of phone calls, but nothing even close to the friendship they'd once shared. She'd been surprised when Lisa had responded to her invitation to attend the Grand's opening night. Amy hoped that it might be the beginning of a new phase in their friendship, but it was early days yet, and she didn't want to force anything.

"We ready?" Quinn asked, offering her his arm.

She smoothed a hand down the front of her dress and glanced quickly around the theatre to make sure everything was as it should be.

The restored seating had been installed last week after being re-chromed and reupholstered in deep burgundy

velvet. Matching velvet curtains draped either side of the
brand new screen, thick gold tasseled ropes holding them
back so that they hung in elegant folds. The floors
gleamed and the wall sconces cast warm light up the soft
cream walls.

She tilted her head back to look at the restored ceiling. Of all her achievements at the Grand, she was most
proud of the ceiling with its stylized depiction of the
heavens. She and the plaster restorer had put in more
than five hundred hours recasting and repairing the
damaged moldings. Now it glowed a brilliant white
with goldleaf highlights and shadows, its lines once
again crisp and clear. It had already attracted the
interest of a number of architectural and interior magazines in advance of the opening, and she'd been approached by a photographer who wanted to document
the Grand in a book celebrating great heritage buildings
in Australia.

She turned to Quinn. "Before we go, there's something I want to say." She reached up and pulled the gorilla
head off so she could see his face. Their guests could wait
a few minutes. This was important.

"I wouldn't be here without you, Quinn Whitfield. You
made my dreams come true. All of them. I love you so
much. Thank you for being so patient and strong and
generous. Thank you for being the best friend I'll ever
have."

His eyes softened. "You're the one who made all this
happen, Ames. You're the one who never lost faith."

His hair was rumpled and he was a gorilla from the
neck down, but her husband was still the best-looking,
sexiest, most wonderful man she'd ever known.

She smiled as she handed him his head back. "If you

play your cards right, we can hook up for a little grooming behavior later on."

Quinn's dark eyes lit with interest. If ever she'd needed it—and she didn't—his unending, apparently inexhaustible desire for her was the ultimate reassurance that her feelings were more than reciprocated.

"Where? When?" he asked.

"How about the projectionist's room, in an hour?"

"Make it forty minutes and you've got a deal."

She stood on her tiptoes and kissed him. For sixteen years she'd fantasized about what it would be like to be loved by Quinn. Reality far surpassed any dream she'd ever had.

"Anytime, anywhere."

She waited until he'd put the gorilla head on, then she took his arm and walked through the archway to greet their guests.

It was going to be a great night.

* * * * *

*Harlequin Intrigue top author Delores Fossen presents
a brand-new series of breathtaking romantic suspense!*
TEXAS MATERNITY: HOSTAGES
The first installment available May 2010:
THE BABY'S GUARDIAN

Shaw cursed and hooked his arm around Sabrina.

Despite the urgency that the deadly gunfire created, he tried to be careful with her, and he took the brunt of the fall when he pulled her to the ground. His shoulder hit hard, but he held on tight to his gun so that it wouldn't be jarred from his hand.

Shaw didn't stop there. He crawled over Sabrina, sheltering her pregnant belly with his body, and he came up ready to return fire.

This was obviously a situation he'd wanted to avoid at all cost. He didn't want his baby in the middle of a fight with these armed fugitives, but when they fired that shot, they'd left him no choice. Now, the trick was to get Sabrina safely out of there.

"Get down," someone on the SWAT team yelled from the roof of the adjacent building.

Shaw did. He dropped lower, covering Sabrina as best he could.

There was another shot, but this one came from a rifleman on the SWAT team. Shaw didn't look up, but he heard the sound of glass being blown apart.

The shots continued, all coming from his men, which meant it might be time to try to get Sabrina to better cover. Shaw glanced at the front of the building.

So that Sabrina's pregnant belly wouldn't be smashed

against the ground, Shaw eased off her and moved her to a sitting position so that her back was against the brick wall. They were close. Too close. And face-to-face.

He found himself staring right into those sea-green eyes.

How will Shaw get Sabrina out?
Follow the daring rescue and the heartbreaking
aftermath in THE BABY'S GUARDIAN
by Delores Fossen, available May 2010 from
Harlequin Intrigue.

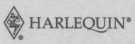

LAURA MARIE ALTOM

The Baby Twins

Stephanie Olmstead has her hands full raising
her twin baby girls on her own. When she runs
into old friend Brady Flynn, she's shocked to find
herself suddenly attracted to the handsome airline
pilot! Will this flyboy be the perfect daddy—
or will he crash and burn?

"LOVE, HOME & HAPPINESS"

www.eHarlequin.com

HAR75309

Former bad boy Sloan Hawkins is back in
Redemption, Oklahoma, to help keep his aunt's
cherished garden thriving and to reconnect with the
girl he left behind, Annie Markham. But when he
discovers his secret child—and that single mother
Annie never stopped loving him—he's determined
that a wedding will take place in the garden
nurtured by faith and love.

REDEMPTION RIVER

Where healing flows...

Look for

The Wedding Garden
by Linda Goodnight

*Available May 2010
wherever you buy books.*

Steeple
Hill®
LI87595

www.SteepleHill.com

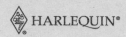
HARLEQUIN®

Showcase

On sale May 11, 2010

Reader favorites from the most talented voices in romance

Save $1.00 on the purchase of 1 or more Harlequin® Showcase books.

SAVE $1.00 on the purchase of 1 or more Harlequin® Showcase books.

Coupon expires Oct 31, 2010. Redeemable at participating retail outlets. Limit one coupon per purchase. Valid in the U.S.A. and Canada only.

52609015

5 65373 00076 2   (8100)0 11651

HSCCOUP0410

COMING NEXT MONTH

Available May 11, 2010